Animal Town

A.D. Ultman

Animal Town is published under Outlier Books, sectionalized division under Di Angelo Publications INC.

OUTLIER BOOKS

an imprint of Di Angelo Publications. Animal Town. Copyright 2021. A.D. Ultman in digital and print distribution in the United States of America.

Di Angelo Publications 4265 San Felipe #1100
Houston, Texas, 77027
www. diangelopublications.com

Library of Congress cataloging-in-publications data

Animal Town
Downloadable via Kindle, iBooks and NOOK.

Library of Congress Registration Paperback

ISBN: 978-1-942549-79-6

Internal Layout: Kimberly James
Cover Illustration: Tamar Volkodav

1. Fiction -- Political
2. Fiction -- Satire
3. Political Science -- Political Ideologies
4. Political Science -- Political Process -- Political Parties

United States of America with int. Distribution.

Animal Town

A.D. Ultman

To the next generation,
may you learn from our mistakes.

CHAPTER 1

"Things have never been better in Animal Town. All animals are free, and animal does not kill animal," the wizened bull bison intones from the front of the classroom in his deep, gravelly voice. As he speaks, his long, graying beard wafts back and forth hypnotically, fixing the children's attention. "But, my dear children, it was not always so." Here he pauses, looking meaningfully about the room. In a desk near the window sits a young whitetail deer, sporting only two antler points; a drab-feathered pheasant hen roosts by the door; a half-grown black bear cub is trying to keep awake in the back row, his head nodding from side to side. Several other young animals—birds and mammals, predators and prey—fill the desks of the one-room schoolhouse, of which the old bison is master. Before continuing his speech, Mr. Hoofman's dim brown eyes meet the blues of a clever young jackrabbit. Floppy, who always sits in the front row, gazes back intently. He loves his old teacher and knows him well enough to recognize the bison is working up to something important.

"No, it was not always so. *Grrumphf.*" Mr. Hoofman grunts, repeating himself to make a point, as is his custom. "Seeing as it is my last day as your schoolmaster before I am 'put out to pasture,' I am going to set aside your regular afternoon courses"—smiles and cheers erupt from the class. Mr. Hoofman sternly waits for them to quiet down, tapping his hoof on the floorboards until it is the only sound in the room—"to give you a special lesson about history. Attitudes are changing on the Animal Town School Board, and your new schoolmaster may teach a different curriculum. So, with my parting words, I urge you to remember the truth about how our town came to be and why all animals are now free. We animals are cursed with selective memories, but when we distort the past, we jeopardize our future."

Again he pauses. His meaning may have escaped some of his duller students—certainly it did Ralph, the bear in the back—but Floppy, nodding gently, seems to understand. Mr. Hoofman continues, "Long ago, in the time before your grandfathers' grandfathers, animals were not free. No, they were not," he sighs, "No, they were not. Before our town was founded, animals lived like savages. Every day was a struggle. They did not know if they would eat or go hungry each day or whether they would live through each night. They knew nothing of the world, and, though they lived in nature, they did not understand it. They made up fantastic stories to try to make sense of things. They believed that invisible animals with magical powers lived among them and caused rain, drought, earthquakes, and lightning."

"Geez, they were dumber than Ralph!" shouts Charlie,

a bright young coyote who serves as the class clown. His classmates break into peals of laughter. Upon hearing his name, Ralph, snoozing with his head propped against the back wall, perks his ears and opens his eyes, startled.

"Who called me dumb?" he growls, half angry, half embarrassed.

"Never mind, never mind," scolds Mr. Hoofman. "Please pay attention, Ralph. And, no, Charlie, they were not dumb; they were *ignorant*. They had the same brains that we have, but they had not learned to use them. They did not know, as we have learned in this very room, that nature is governed by laws that animals can discover. They did not know, as you do, that the scientific method can be used to learn these laws, as well as many other facts about the world, and that this knowledge can help animals make better lives for themselves.

"But that is hardly the worst of it, dear children. In their ignorance, our ancestors knew nothing of the Big Bang, where planets, stars, and galaxies came from, or even that there are other planets and galaxies. Instead, each species believed that the Earth is the center of a universe that an invisible, magic animal made especially for them. Many species even believed that one such invisible animal used his magical powers to spy on their every move and listen to their thoughts! And if that magic animal didn't like what they did and thought, even when they were alone, he would torture them for all eternity! Now, aren't you glad we know better?"

"Isn't that what ol' Mr. Scratch is always going on about?" asks Goldy, a young gopher with shining fur, plaintively.

"Huummrrr," replies Mr. Hoofman, "I can't well say, as I have never been to his foxhole, err *temple*"—a few chuckles from the class—"but it may well be. It may well be…

"Not only were they ignorant about nature," the old bison continues, "but they were also ignorant about themselves. They did not know, as that poster nicely illustrates…" Mid-sentence, Mr. Hoofman points his forehoof toward the wall where hangs a poster depicting hierarchically organized extinct and living creatures. At the top it reads, *The Descent of Animal.* "…that all animals share a common ancestor sometime in the distant past. For example, as we have learned, it is quite true that you, Sylvester, though you are a wolf, and you, Cassie, though you are a sheep, have the same great-great-great-great-great-great-great-great-great-great-great-great-great-*great*-grandmother!" Laughter again bursts from the class, and Mr. Hoofman smiles indulgently, pleased that his humor has hit its mark. "You may laugh," he says, "but it's quite true, quite true."

He continues after the laughter has quieted, "But our ancestors did not know it was true, and so *every* species thought it was special and the best species of all. What's more, far from being free, each species was pitted against every other in a brutal struggle to survive in a world where food was scarce and only the strongest, smartest, or luckiest succeeded." Mr. Hoofman looks grimly around the room before lowering his voice still further to say, "Animals even...*ate* each other. *Grrumphf.*"

The children engage in a collective gasp, sucking the air out of the room. They know vaguely of the time, long ago, when animals ate each other, but it is rarely spoken about in public. Given the harmony that prevails among animals today, it is difficult for them to imagine.

"That's disgusting!" shrieks Becky, in her sharp pheasant voice. Other children stare, wide-eyed.

"I know, Becky. I know," rejoins Mr. Hoofman. "But that was the only way predators could survive before animals learned how to farm: they had to hunt. Meanwhile, prey had to wander far and wide to gather enough food to survive, and they were constantly on the brink of starvation. Only after animals learned how to farm, and this was relatively recently, did animals of the same species begin living together in towns and cities. Even after they learned to farm, animal still killed animal in wars over land, resources, or magical stories. Pred killed pred, prey killed prey, and they killed each other. I'm afraid our animal ancestors' lives were miserable, laborious, and short. Yes, nature was red in hoof and paw, red in hoof and paw, you might say."

"I'm glad we know better now," says Floppy, looking shaken.

"Don't worry, Floppy. I'd never eat *you*. You'd taste terrible!" jokes Charlie, with a wry smile, causing Floppy and the rest of the class to chuckle lightheartedly. The two are good friends.

"It's hardly a joking matter, Charlie," chides Mr. Hoofman. "It certainly wasn't to our ancestors.

"Anyway, after a long period during which all species struggled against one another, with neither pred nor prey gaining the upper paw or hoof, something suddenly changed. The predators learned to use the scientific method to understand nature, and this enabled them to rapidly acquire far more knowledge than animals ever had. Preds used the knowledge to create new technology that gave them a huge advantage over prey for the first time. Then, using their powerful technology, preds spread out across the land as never before, conquering and killing prey as they went. They soon reached the land where Animal Town now stands, and the pred diseases and advanced weapons they carried all but wiped out the prey that once lived here. Then, seeing how they had conquered the prey, many of the preds came to believe that they were superior to the prey and that it was their destiny to rule over them."

"Wait, didn't you say *all* species thought they were the best?" This from Charlie.

"Yes. That's true, Charlie. Long ago *all* species thought they were the best, and beyond Animal Town many still do; but this was the first time the pred species thought of themselves as a single superior group and of the prey species as a single inferior group.

"You see, class," Mr. Hoofman continues, "The preds misunderstood why they were able to conquer the prey. They thought it was simply *because they were predators*. As predators, they assumed they were entitled to more freedom than prey and felt justified in ruling over them. They forgot that they, too, were once ignorant and weak and that they had often been conquered and killed by prey in the past. The preds failed to see that *it was their knowledge that gave them freedom*, their knowledge that gave them freedom."

Mr. Hoofman pauses for a moment and sees flickers of understanding flash across a few of the children's faces. Others remain dim.

"You see children, unfortunately, knowledge can be used for bad purposes as well as good, and the preds often used it for bad, I'm afraid."

By now some of the pred children are growing uncomfortable with Mr. Hoofman's lecture. They aren't sure, but it sounds to them like Mr. Hoofman is calling preds bad. Ralph, Charlie, and several others exchange dubious glances. Ralph finally speaks up. "Aaarh, but, uh, Mr. Hoofman, didn't the preds, you know, share their techno-, techno-ology and knowledge and stuff with the prey? I mean, prey seem to know everything that preds do now."

"Ha, we know more than Ralph anyway!" says the young whitetail buck, cocky now that his antlers have sprouted. The other prey children laugh.

"*Uuuurm*," Mr. Hoofman groans. "Yes, Ralph; you're right. Eventually they did share, and prey learned for themselves, too; and now animals live longer, healthier, and more prosperous lives than ever before as a result. Today all animals are free, as I have said. But I am still talking about the past, so please don't be offended. You and the other preds have no reason to feel bad about the actions of your ancestors, and prey ancestors are not innocent either. Besides, as I was just saying, if we look back far enough, we all have the same ancestors anyway." The children quiet down.

"Now where was I? Oh, yes: one of the bad things preds used their knowledge and technology for, *in the past*, was to force some prey species to work against their will, as slaves. Long ago, many prey were stolen from their families, carried across the ocean, and made to work for the preds of Animal Town. Of course, dear children, it is important to remember that different species had enslaved one another for all of animal history—prey enslaved prey, preds enslaved preds, and they enslaved each other—but seldom had so many animals been enslaved so far from their homes. To make matters worse, back in their homeland, prey species enslaved other prey to sell to the preds and even kept slaves themselves. So you see, Ralph? Slavery is a black mark on *all* of animal history. No species is innocent."

At this Ralph and some of the other preds grin smugly.

"Anyway, this went on for a long time, and many prey died as a result. Eventually, though, knowledge was used for good. Right here in Animal Town, some of the preds began to understand that all animals must be free. They learned that prey animals are conscious and care about their lives in just the same way that pred animals do. Understanding this, they knew that no animal of any species has a right to enslave an animal of any other, or his own for that matter. They tried to end slavery and set the prey free. But many of the preds had not yet learned that all animals have an equal right to freedom and wanted to keep the prey enslaved. So the preds fought a terrible war among themselves, with one side fighting for knowledge and freedom and the other for ignorance and slavery. Thankfully, the side of knowledge won the war, but not before a great many preds, and some prey as well, died fighting for the cause. Slavery was finally abolished, but prey still weren't entirely free. No, they still weren't free."

"Yes, yes. We remember this part of the story," several children murmur. Though the period of hunting and gathering is seldom spoken of, the children have learned much about Animal Town's recent past.

"Good," says Mr. Hoofman. "See that you do remember. And would someone from the class like to tell us what happened next?" A pause follows as Mr. Hoofman looks about the room. The young animals shift their weight anxiously. "Anyone?" Another pause. "How about you, Floppy?"

Floppy shifts in his chair, gathers himself, and says, "The prey weren't slaves anymore, but they weren't really part of Animal Town yet either. Because they had to live in separate areas and go to separate schools and stuff. And they couldn't go to town meetings or vote for mayor."

"Very good, very good, that's right, Floppy. And then what happened?"

"Well, it took, like, a long time, but finally Mr. Prince convinced everyone that prey deserve to be free too, and they should be able to go to the same schools as preds and not be separated or anything, and that they should be able to vote for mayor, too." Floppy speaks quickly but confidently.

"Good. That's basically right, but it took more than convincing, I'd say. Some of the preds had to be forced to accept prey and new laws had to be passed, but, yes, now prey can live wherever they want, and vote for mayor, and we can all go to Lyle Luckson Sr. All Animal School together. Yes, children, all animals are free, and it's been that way since long before you were born. Why, we even have a prey mayor!"

With Mr. Hoofman's affirmation of the town credo, the tension between his pred and prey students dissipates. Tails wag gently and the children smile at one another.

"And so, dear children," Mr. Hoofman concludes, "on my last day as your schoolmaster, I beg you to remember all I have taught you. Remember how our ancestors struggled in ignorance and darkness before knowledge lit the way. Remember that no animal is guilty of the crimes of his grandfathers and that no species is innocent.

Remember that all animals are brothers and sisters, and all have an equal right to freedom. Mark well the lesson of history: animal freedom depends on knowledge. When we turn our tails on the truth, we sow the seeds of our own destruction.

CHAPTER 2

The school day over and the weekend begun, the children trundle down the schoolhouse steps into the crisp, mid-winter air. Many do so with mixed emotions. They are sad to see their old teacher go, but, at the same time, they are excited by the contents of his farewell lecture. To think of it: invisible animals with magic powers spying and torturing; animals eating each other and living like savages; species killing species and enslaving each other. It is a lot for their young minds to handle. Some would have preferred not to be reminded of their brutal past, but they all agree they are glad to be living now, when all animals are free and when animal does not kill animal.

Floppy, especially, is unsettled. He will miss Mr. Hoofman more than most of the children, and his lecture made a deeper impression on the young hare. Like the others, he is repulsed by the thought of preds hunting and eating prey, but what most concerns Floppy is the idea that sprouted in his mind when Mr. Hoofman mentioned Lyle Luckson Sr. There was something discordant about hearing Mr. Luckson's name just before the town credo, "all animals are free". At that moment, the seed of a perennial idea, long-dormant, then budded in the fertile soil of

Floppy's mind. The thought is still too underdeveloped for him to express consciously or hold firmly, but Floppy is sure there is something that sets the weasel apart from the other animals. *Might he have more freed—*

"You're sure gonna miss that old bull, aye, Floppy?" Charlie shouts as he springs from the top of the steps and pounces playfully onto Floppy, knocking him down.

"Come on, Charlie. Knock it off." He chastises, righting himself, and brushing the dust from his pants. "I'm trying to think."

"Oh, you're always thinking. You know, you think too much for your own good."

"On the contrary," says Floppy, affecting haughtiness, "other animals do not think enough."

The two fall in together and start walking toward their family dens.

"Yeah, whatever you say. Anyway, I bet you were thinking you wish you were a pred!"

"What makes you say that?" asks Floppy.

"Because we conquered all the animals, of course," Charlie says, only half-joking, sticking his snout in the air.

"Weren't you listening, Charlie? *You* didn't conquer anything. It was knowledge that conquered, and it was your grandfathers' grandfathers' knowledge at that. And they used it rather badly at first, you may recall."

"Yeah, yeah, I remember. How about the magical animals causing lighting and rain and stuff? What a bunch of rot, aye? Hey, that reminds me. Let's play a little pawball on the field by ol' Scratch's 'temple.' We can hassle the old coot a bit while we're there."

The two friends make their way towards the field together, as is their afterschool custom. In spring and summer, the field blooms lustily with wildflowers, making it a popular picnic and recreation ground. In winter it becomes an empty plain of flat, brown grass—perfect for pawball. After a few minutes' walk, they arrive.

At one end of the field is a series of low earthen mounds. Dug into one is the "Great Predator Temple of Animal Town," so called by the red fox who excavated and presides over it, Mr. Scratch. Though animals still use the requisite traditional names to describe their homes—den, burrow, nest, etc.—most of the residents of Animal Town are by now living in houses made of wood or brick, equipped with all the modern conveniences one expects to find in an educated and prosperous society. The Temple, however, really is little more than a large foxhole, with dirt floors and walls and space within for perhaps ten stooping animals. Mr. Scratch's poverty and refusal to work for a living require him to live in the old way, though he would prefer the comforts of modern life.

The rusticity of the Temple is of little concern to the

residents of Animal Town, at any rate, for none have visited in many years. Indeed, little is known about the stories Mr. Scratch once told there, but there are rumors that, in his younger days, he had regularly delivered fiery sermons to a few old preds about a magic father animal, eternal damnation, and paradise. Today, though, his muzzle is grayed with advanced age, and he seldom has the energy to sermonize, much less a congregation to preach to. He is merely indulged by the townsanimals as a harmless eccentric.

There is no sign of Mr. Scratch as the spry young animals knock around the pawball that Charlie "borrowed" from the schoolhouse. Though the several species of Animal Town have converged in size since they have been living together, Charlie is bigger and stronger than Floppy. He often muscles Floppy off the ball, but Floppy's superior speed and agility often enable him to dodge and bound past Charlie. They play with the pure joy of youthful friendship until late afternoon when the early sunset makes it difficult to see.

A gust of cold winter wind descends on the field from the north as a dark figure appears in the twilight, trotting toward them. It is Mr. Scratch, returning from begging alms in Town Square, his only means of subsistence. His yellow eyes flash and then narrow when he sees the boys playing. They have not yet noticed the sly fox.

"You had best be getting on home, boys, or you'll be late for dinner!" Mr. Scratch barks. His voice startles them, causing Charlie to misplay the ball, which rolls away. Mr. Scratch eyes Floppy, and under his breath, he mutters, "Or maybe you'll *become* dinner."

Seeing it is Mr. Scratch, whom he wanted to poke, Charlie retorts, "What business is it of yours, you mangy old fox?"

Before Mr. Scratch can respond, Floppy intervenes, "Don't worry about it, Charlie. He's right anyway. I should get going. My parents hate it when I'm late for family dinner."

"Alright, alright. You're no fun. Good game today, and say 'hi' to your folks for me."

Floppy springs away, ignoring Mr. Scratch. Charlie trots after the pawball, which rolled in the fox's direction. He gathers it and begins to turn toward home.

"Just a minute there, young pred. I'd like a word with you." A crooked half-smile curls across Mr. Scratch's lips, revealing his dulled canine teeth.

Charlie is brazen but still kind, so he stops to hear the old fox out, feeling a little sorry for him. "What?" he says, flatly.

"What's your name, pup?"

"Charlie."

"My, what a handsome and strong young pred you are, Charlie. Such a shame for your strength to go to waste."

"What are you talking about?" asks Charlie, suspecting Mr. Scratch of lechery.

"You really shouldn't be mixing with that silly little rabbit. It's unnatural. You'll start acting like prey and thinking like prey, and pretty soon you'll be as silly and weak as them."

"I still don't know what you're talking about, but Floppy is probably the smartest kid in my class."

"Ha, that's pride!" barks Mr. Scratch, angrily. "Those animals think they're so smart with their science and their books, but they don't know a damn thing. They don't know the *word*."

"What *word*?" Tiring of the conversation, Charlie shuffles his paws impatiently.

"The word of our Great Pred Father, in whose image you and I were made, my pup. He has commanded us that pred and prey are not to live together. That living together causes preds to weaken and die."

"Well, I feel fine, and I have lots of prey friends. Anyway, I gotta go. Goodnight, sir." Charlie turns and trots away, heading west, toward the edge of town, where his mother is waiting to drive him into the wind and farms of the countryside.

He has covered only a few meters when the cagey fox calls after him, "You are a master species, Charlie! Remember that!" But the wind catches his words and whisks them from the young coyote's ears. Mr. Scratch stares at Charlie's silhouette as it recedes into the distance and stands for a moment, brooding. The darkness of night falls around his matted fur. Then old Scratch enters the Great Predator Temple of Animal Town and lies down in the dirt, alone.

From the field, Floppy heads south, towards the town center. His family den, a modest but orderly two-room shanty, lies among those of Animal Town's working prey. Though they have the right to live anywhere in Animal Town, most of the prey cluster together in a neighborhood not far from the Luckson Shiny Rock Mine, where they work to excavate and polish the stones which serve as the town's currency.

Arriving at his den, Floppy overhears his parents' voices within. They sound anxious. He pauses to listen, bending his ear to the crack between the door and threshold, caused by a shifting foundation.

"What if Junior won't take the bribe? I don't want our kits to end up on the street," he hears his mother say.

"He'll take it, Lil. Don't worry. Our neighbors have all done it," replies his father, Jack.

"Your parents should never have sold to Mr. Luckson. We wouldn't have this problem if we owned this place."

"Believe me, Lil, I know. But what could they do? Dad got the black lung. It was either sell the house and pay the doctors or keep it and watch him die. Mom did what she had to. She worked herself to death at that mine, trying to keep our family afloat."

Floppy's grandfather died before he was born. He has faint memories of his grandmother, her paws rigid and arthritic from years of rock polishing. He presses his ear to the crack.

"I'm sorry, Jack. You're right. It's really Mr. Luckson we should blame. He doesn't pay us any more to mine his rocks than he paid your parents, but the rent keeps going up every year."

"If only there were somewhere else we could go, but that weasel has bought up practically the whole town. He won't even make repairs anymore. The roof leaks, the windows are drafty, and this place is starting to tilt like a funhouse." Jack sighs heavily.

"We're just going to have to keep working double shifts. We'll catch up in a few months," says Lil, affecting optimism. "At least little Lepu is feeling better."

"And thank goodness for that," says Jack. "Those hospital bills were killing us. Come on; let's set the table for dinner. Floppy should be home any minute."

Floppy waits in silence, considering what he has heard. He knows his family does not have many shiny rocks but, judging from his parents' conversation, things are worse than he realized. It had not occurred to him that his sister's illness threatened to ruin his family's finances. *I wish there was something I could do*, he thinks.

A minute passes. Floppy puts on a smile, turns the door handle, and bursts into the den as if he has not been eavesdropping. "Hiya, Dad. Hiya, Mom," he says.

"Hi, Floppy. Welcome home," his parents respond in unison.

"Drop your backpack in your room and tell your sister it's time for dinner—we're having peas," Jack says, placing a steaming bowl of legumes on the table.

Lil extracts her infant sons from their crib by the fireplace and places them in wooden highchairs. Floppy and Lepu return from their room, and soon the family of six is seated together at table, a picture of working-class domesticity.

Many of Floppy's neighbors have faced hardships of their own and have likewise sold their homes to Mr. Luckson. Thus, though they have the right to live anywhere, most prey in Animal Town can barely afford to live where they are.

Similar stories of struggle can be heard in the countryside west of town, where Charlie's family lives. Like most of the preds of Animal Town, they live on a farm where they raise the crops that feed the town.

And, like most preds, they, too, pay rent to Mr. Luckson. Charlie's family specializes in growing the protein-rich plants that preds eat in lieu of meat. Presently, the coyote family is at table, eating some such plants.

"The loan will cover us until the fall, as long as he doesn't raise the rent again, but we'd better hope for a bumper crop this year if we're ever gonna pay back Mr. Luckson," says Charlie's father, his mouth full of food.

"I could plant a bigger garden. Maybe we could sell some home-grown veggies in town to make a few extra rocks," offers his mother.

"That's a good idea, but what we really need is another paw around here to help us get ready for planting season. Do you have any classmates looking for an afterschool job, Charlie? Hard workers, I mean."

Charlie shrugs.

"Well, think about it."

Floppy and Charlie hungrily devour their meager dinners in their meager dwellings after their spirited game of pawball. Outside their dens, the sky is covered in the blackness of a new moon, marking the completion of the lunar cycle by which Mr. Luckson manages his properties. For both prey and predator, town and countryside, rent has come due, and Mr. Luckson's agents will soon be coming to collect.

CHAPTER 3

"Junior! Where are you, Junior? And why aren't you out collecting rent? Didn't you see the new moon? You could at least do the only job you have around here!" Mr. Luckson's agitated voice resounds through the grand hall of his mansion, overlooking Animal Town Lake. As if in response, loud music and the pitter-patter of dancing weasel paws tumble down the staircase and meet his pert ears. The commotion indicates that his son, Lyle Jr., is in the midst of one of his frequent debauches.

Realizing that Junior is again partying instead of working, Mr. Luckson cannot help being disappointed in his son.

His family's history has taught him that land ownership is the key to wealth, power, and freedom. His grandfather weasel homesteaded in Animal Town's early days and dug a burrow next to the river rapids which once skirted it. When the town built a dam on his land, he grew rich on payments for the electricity and crop irrigation the river generated. His grandfather used the accumulated wealth to buy up the countryside surrounding the town. Mr. Luckson's father inherited the land, and a few years later a lode of shiny rocks was discovered deep within it. He used the wealth generated from the farmers' rent to build the Luckson Shiny Rock Mine. Mr. Luckson inherited his grandfather's farmland and his father's mine in his turn, and he increased the family fortune still further by buying up most of the property and homes in town.

Junior stands to inherit his forebears' land and wealth, to be sure, but he has not inherited their work ethic or business acumen. Mr. Luckson fears that he will squander the patrimony that he, his father, and grandfather have so steadily accumulated. He was raised to be keenly aware of the old adage, "It takes three generations to ruin a family fortune." Mr. Luckson is confident he will not be the one to do the ruining, but he has his doubts about the fourth generation Junior represents.

Sighing audibly, Mr. Luckson gives his cane, coat, and hat to his bison butler in the foyer and mounts the ornate marble staircase, with lush red carpet down its center. At the top, he turns to the east wing of the mansion where Junior has his rooms and from which the festive commotion emanates. The door of his son's reception room is ajar, and Mr. Luckson slips in silently.

He is greeted by the sight of his son, naked from the waist up so that his large belly protrudes obscenely, dancing provocatively with a scantily clad young lady under each arm. Mr. Luckson recognizes the two jill weasels from the social club where the wealthy residents of Animal Town gather, and where they sell their attention to the highest bidder. They have not noticed him.

"See girls?" Junior boasts, "I told you I'm the best dancer in Animal Town! Some animals say I'm the best dancer in the world!" As he brags, Junior's hind paws trample awkwardly over those of the jills, and his forepaws grope them shamelessly.

Mr. Luckson's face screws up as if he has caught a whiff of an unpleasant odor. "Blast it, Junior! Didn't you see the new moon? You're supposed to be collecting rent from the prey in town tonight, or don't you care about the family business?"

Hearing his father over the din at last, Junior is too distracted by the ladies to be concerned with his duty. "I can't leave the girls now, Daddy. I've already paid for the night. Why don't you just have that brown-nosed ewe collect the rent instead?" he says while continuing to gyrate between them. The ewe to whom he refers is Camilla, a bighorn sheep in his father's employ.

"Camilla is busy collecting rent from the preds in the countryside. Besides, you know I don't like prey collecting from prey or preds collecting from preds. Blast it! If you're too busy with these tarts to do your job, then I guess I'll have to do it myself." Mr. Luckson's voice rises in anger as he scolds his negligent son. "But you had better learn to take responsibility if you mean to run the family business one day!" With this he turns on his paws and leaves the room, slamming the door behind him.

The wooden thud of the door against its frame punctuates the gaudy music. Hurt by his father's words, the bulbous weasel ceases dancing and the boisterous grin fades from his face. Despite his flippant behavior, deep down Junior is desperate for his senior's approval. Indeed, part of the reason he is so boastful is to cover up the fact that he feels inferior to his illustrious forebear. Further, he admires his father's wealth and influence in Animal Town and wants them for himself. In fact, wealth, power, fame, and females are the only things he cares about, and he knows he must keep on his father's good side if he is to have them. Nevertheless, he is too conceited to let the jills know his true feelings. He regains his cocksure demeanor and continues boasting after his father is out of earshot.

"Don't let that old weasel bother you, girls. He won't be around forever, and when he's gone all this will be mine." He makes a sweeping gesture with his forepaw. "I am going to be the greatest, most powerful animal in the history of Animal Town! You'll see!"

Mr. Luckson sets out in his son's stead to collect rent from the prey of Animal Town. He is escorted by Officer Furman, a black bear who pads his meager police salary by acting as Mr. Luckson's private security. Under the cover of the new moon, they make their way to the shantytown. Upon arriving, Mr. Luckson knocks on each door and puts out his paw, broking no excuses while

Officer Furman looks sternly over his shoulder.

Halfway through his rounds, Mr. Luckson's mood, already far from pleasant as a result of the encounter with his son, has turned sourer still. He rarely sets paw among the shanties, for he loathes mixing with the poor of Animal Town. He feels he is somehow tainted by the squalor in which they live, that the dirt and stink of poverty seeps into his fur and chokes him. He prefers not to be reminded of the gulf between his life and theirs. What's more, he detests hearing their pleadings for forbearance, about how this little gosling is sick, how that buck has been injured on the job, or how cold the den has been this winter. "A tenant's first duty is to his landlord," he tells the prey, "and animals must manage their affairs accordingly."

At length, the weasel and the bear make their way to Floppy's den, wherein the jackrabbit family has just finished dinner. Mr. Luckson raps his gold-handled cane harshly on the door, which is slightly ajar in its frame, allowing a winter draft to slip through. A moment later the door swings open, and Floppy's father appears, holding a basket of food. Before he can say a word, Mr. Luckson thrusts a paw into the jackrabbit's face and says, curtly, "Rent due: fifty grams of shiny rocks."

Seeing that it is Mr. Luckson Sr. himself, escorted by Furman, and not his perfidious son, Jack's whiskers droop despondently. He and his wife have just paid little Lepu's doctor bills, and, as a result, they have only half the rent this month. In the hope of being granted an extension, they have rationed their meals for weeks and traded the leftovers for predator food. The rumor among the prey is that Junior is a glutton and can be persuaded to accept food for himself in lieu of rent for his father.

"G-g-good evening, Mr. Luckson." Jack stammers, "W-w-won't you come in?"

"No time for that. I have many more tenants yet to see tonight: fifty grams of shiny rocks, *if you please.*"

Jack looks furtively at Lil. She is on the verge of tears. Floppy and Lepu peek through the cracked door of their room; their twin baby brothers rock obliviously in their crib, next to the narrow fireplace. Jack takes a deep breath before turning to face Mr. Luckson again. "You see, sir, our daughter has been sick, and, well..."

"Enough of that," the weasel interrupts. "How much have you got?"

Jack startles. "T-t-twenty-five g-g-grams, sir," he manages to say, producing a tiny pouch from his pocket.

Mr. Luckson snatches the pouch and tosses it to Furman. "Late payment means double rent next month, rabbit. And see that you are not late again, or it will become Officer Furman's concern." At this the bear's upper lip pulls back slightly, revealing the points of his fangs. He emits a low growl.

"Oh, thank you, sir. We won't be late again. Please accept this gift basket as a t-t-token of our gratitude. We chose it especially for you."

The wealthy weasel sends a clipped, high-pitched bark in Furman's direction, who snaps the basket from Jack's paws.

"Maybe," the bear mutters, "you could afford your rent if you didn't have so many kits." He swings the door closed, scraping its paint with his claws.

Mr. Luckson and Officer Furman leave Floppy's den and head for the next row of shanties. As they turn down the alley, the landlord commands, "Keep an eye on that jackrabbit, Furry. We may have to make an example of him. And get rid of that stinking basket—to think of me eating their filthy food!"

"Yes, sir, Mr. Luckson, sir!" Furman tosses the basket into a nearby dumpster. His beady black eyes remain fixed on it for several seconds as they continue down the alley. The burly black bear regrets wasting food that might have fed his hungry family.

Meanwhile, Camilla, the bighorn sheep ewe, has been driving across the countryside collecting rent from the preds. Over her dusky brown fur, she wears a stylish business suit, and her rear hoofs squeeze precariously into sensible heels.

She makes her rounds among the pred farmhouses, ignoring pleas for rent relief similar to those Mr. Luckson hears from the prey. *I'm sick of their excuses.* She thinks to herself, pulling into the driveway at her last stop. *If I can make it in Animal Town, these preds can too.*

Camilla has indeed made it in Animal Town. Given Junior's incompetence, she has become Mr. Luckson's right paw animal, a position of great influence. Moreover, she commands a respectable fortune of her own, bequeathed by her deceased parents. Both immigrants from the East who became prominent professors at Animal Town University, Camilla's parents were able to take full advantage of the freedom Animal Town offers. From them she was fortunate to inherit not only wealth and good genes, which gave her financial security and a superior sheep brain, but also the work ethic and grit that set her apart from Junior and which have won her Mr. Luckson's favor.

She parks her expensive car in the tenants' driveway. A sign hanging over the garage reads, *Fleischbauer.* Walking to the front door with a confident bearing, yet another privilege passed down from her parents is on display: Camilla is strikingly good looking.

The middle-aged ewe knocks, and moments later the door creaks open.

"Help you?" says a gruff grey wolf; tall, broad, and shirtless in his soiled blue jeans.

"I hope so, Fleischbauer," replies Camilla, unfazed. "I'm sure you saw the new moon. That means 100 grams of shiny rocks for your beneficent landlord."

"Benifi-what?"

"Benifi-*cent*. It means—"

"Oh, I don't care what it means. Just take your rocks and go," says the wolf with contempt. He tosses a bag of shiny rocks at Camilla's hooves.

"Happily. Until next month then." Camilla scoops up the bag and turns on her hooves.

"Ah, about that," says the wolf, placing a paw on her shoulder and turning her to face him again. "My tractor is on the fritz again, and it'll cost me a pile to have it fixed. I'm gonna need an extension on my rent next month. Luckson knows I'm good for it."

"That may be," Camilla responds, brushing the enormous paw from her shoulder. "But you answer to me, Fleischbauer, and I say the repairs will have to wait. A tenant's first duty is to his landlord, and animals must manage their affairs accordingly."

CHAPTER 4

Floppy has not had a restful weekend. His father's encounter with Mr. Luckson has weighed heavily on his mind. He is old enough, and clever enough to know that his parents must work even longer hours at the mine in order to earn next month's double rent, and that means he will have extra duties around the den. He will have little time for pawball with Charlie after school. Familial worries exacerbate Floppy's unease regarding Mr. Hoofman's retirement and the contents of his farewell lecture. All weekend he has been thinking about Mr. Luckson and what it means to be free. Mr. Hoofman said it is knowledge that makes animals free, and Floppy understands that Animal Town's freedom and prosperity do, indeed, depend on knowledge. He knows that knowledge cured the diseases that once took the old and weak, saved the mothers who once died in childbirth, and fed the animals who once starved.

Nevertheless, Floppy cannot shake the thought that how much knowledge an animal has isn't the only thing that makes him more or less free. After all, in the way most children do, he believes his father is as knowledgeable as any animal in town, except maybe Mr. Hoofman or

Mayor Middleton, and yet he must work at the mine to earn rocks to pay Mr. Luckson rent. Mr. Luckson doesn't seem to Floppy any more knowledgeable than his father, and yet he does not have to work; he only collects other animals' shiny rocks. Floppy is beginning to think that true freedom requires not only knowledge but something more. The sprout of an idea has become a seedling.

Other thoughts occupy his classmates' minds as they enter the schoolhouse together on a frosty winter morning. Some have already begun to forget Mr. Hoofman's final lecture. Mostly they are excited to learn who will replace him as their new schoolmaster. As they doff their winter garments at the back of the classroom, they chatter excitedly amongst themselves.

"I hope it's a girl," squawks a fledgling bald eagle with mottled brown feathers.

"I hope it's a boy," rejoins another student.

"I hope she's funny," Charlie offers.

"I hope she's pretty," says Ralph.

"Hey, what happened to the posters?" asks Goldy the gopher.

The chatter stops as the children look around the room. In their excitement, they failed to notice, but the schoolroom has indeed changed. Above the chalkboard, at the front of the room, there had once been several posters depicting Animal Town's founding fathers. Among them were the first pred to explore the region where the town lies—a bold and ruthless weasel with greasy black fur—the first three mayors of Animal Town—respectively, a tall, regal mountain lion, an aged bear with curly white fur, and a rather philosophic looking fox; also missing is the stoic countenance of Mayor Blinkin, the wiry eagle who led the war to end slavery. In their place is a large portrait of Mayor Middleton—the current mayor looking stately with his black pronghorns. The portraits on the science wall, which used to be above the animal evolution poster, have likewise been removed. The inventor of the light bulb—a wise and vainglorious wolf; antibiotic medicine—a wily coyote; and the computer—a thin, awkward bear—are gone. In their place hangs a large portrait of Marcus Prince, the saintly bison who finally convinced Animal Town that prey must have the same freedom as preds, long before the children were born.

But that is not all that has changed.

"Never mind the posters. Where's my desk?" asks Sylvester, the wolf who usually sits in the front row, next to Floppy.

"Hey, yeah," joins Becky. "Where's mine?"

"Too bad for you! Mine's in the right place!" calls Ralph smugly, from the back row.

Just then, their new schoolmaster enters the room, walking purposefully, her head held high. She is a young, barely adult golden gopher. On her nose rest stylish, black-rimmed spectacles that appear not to have lenses. About her body is draped an oversized sweater. On her face is a stern expression.

"Preds in the back. Prey in the front," she calls out forcefully, in her squeaky rodent voice. "You shall find your desks have been arranged accordingly."

She walks to the chalkboard and begins writing. Meanwhile, the children use the affixed nametags to locate their desks and take their seats. Whereas before they had been intermixed, with each student sitting where he or she pleased, the prey now occupy the front two rows, while the preds occupy the back two.

At the front of the room, in quick motions and excellent pawwriting, their new schoolmaster chalks out her name: *D-r.-G-r-e-e-n-b-i-t-t-e-r*. Underneath, she writes the town credo: *All animals are free.* Then she turns to face the class, opens her mouth as if to speak, but says nothing and returns to the chalkboard. As the children watch in hushed expectation, she adds, in larger print: *But some animals are freer than others.* Then she underlines the phrase with a quick sweeping motion and caps it with an emphatic period.

Upon reading the addition to the town credo, Floppy's ears perk up. It seems to confirm the idea that has been growing in his mind these past few days. *Of course*, he thinks to himself. *Some animals are freer than others. Maybe that's why my parents have to work and Mr. Luckson doesn't: maybe weasels are freer than jackrabbits.* He sits bolt upright and listens with rapt attention to what comes next.

"Good morning, class. I am Dr. Greenbitter, your new schoolmaster," says the modish gopher, facing the students again and smiling widely at the first two rows. Her smile exposes her long, gnawing teeth, yellowed at the center.

"Good morning, Dr. Greenbitter," several respond, halfheartedly.

"I have been so looking forward to this day. Mr. Hoofman has spoken very highly of you, and, from your academic records, it appears that you have great potential. I intend to help you realize that potential, especially those of you who have been marginalized in the past."

Charlie, wanting to establish himself with his new teacher and also genuinely curious, already has a forepaw in the air, waving impatiently.

"I see you…," Dr. Greenbitter pauses as she confirms his name by the desk tag, "Charlie, but does anyone else have a question first, someone from the first two rows perhaps?" She smiles enticingly at her prey students. After a moment's hesitation, a lamb raises her hoof. "Yes… Cassie. What is your question?"

"Welcome to Luckson All Animal School, Dr. Greenbitter. I was wondering, what are you a doctor of? I thought doctors worked at hospitals. My dad is a doctor, and that's where he works," she bleats.

"An excellent question, young ewe, thank you for it. I recently completed a doctorate in prey studies at Animal Town University. You see, Cassie, some doctors study science or medicine, but I studied *critical species theory*. When Mr. Hoofman announced his retirement, the school board thought it was time someone like me woke you students up. So, here I am."

Believing she has given a satisfactory answer, Dr. Greenbitter then asks, "Are there any other questions from the prey?" Charlie's paw remains in the air.

The students are confused. They have never heard of prey studies or critical species theory and do have questions, but they reflexively follow the practice established by Mr. Hoofman of asking questions in order. Charlie's paw has been raised for some time, and they think it would be rude to skip him again. Floppy, too, holds his tongue for this reason, though he wants to ask about what Dr. Greenbitter has written on the chalkboard. Polite silence reigns for several seconds, as Charlie's paw begins to flag.

"Very well, what is *your* question, Charlie?" Dr. Greenbitter finally asks.

"Whathappenedtoalltheposters?" Charlie bursts in one breath, as if the question had been pressurized inside him, like steam in a teapot.

"I took them down."

"Why?" Charlie and several other students ask, automatically.

"Because the animals they depicted were pred supremacists."

The students look quizzically at one another. *Pred supremacist* is another phrase they have not heard before.

"What's a pred suprema-premacist?" chirps Becky, the ring-necked pheasant.

Dr. Greenbitter frowns, her whiskers sagging at sharp angles from her puffy cheeks. "If you do not already know, then it is high time you learned. Pred supremacy is the ideology upon which Animal Town was founded and which dominates it to this day. Its core is the belief that predators are superior to prey and ought to rule them. Animal Town's founding fathers were all pred supremacists, and so I took their posters down. You see, class, pred culture is defined by greed, aggression, and *specism*. That is why preds murdered and enslaved prey wherever they went. It's in their DNA."

A few hooves and paws rise.

"Yes, Goldy?"

"What's specism, Dr Greenbitter?"

"Traditionally, specism is when pred species believe in their superiority and oppress prey species. Specism can be far more subtle, however. It may even seem to be invisible, but I assure you, it is everywhere, all the time. It is present wherever preds have more power than prey and wherever there is a disparity between them. For example, the fact that pred students in this class have higher average grades than prey students is solely the result of specism. That is why I rearranged your desks and will always call on prey first. By seating prey in front and calling on you first, we take one small step toward reversing the systemic specism that has caused prey to score lower. You see, Goldy, because pred culture is fundamentally specist, we must confront it head-on."

The whole class is listening intently to their new teacher, startled by her accusatory tone. Ears stand at attention and eyes open wide. Ralph raises his paw, along with several other preds.

"Yes… Ralph. What is your question?"

"But Mr. Hoofman taught us prey species used to think *they* were superior. So are prey specists too?"

"No, Ralph," replies Dr. Greenbitter, firmly. "*There is no such thing as reverse specism.* Specism requires power, and prey do not have power. Therefore, prey cannot be specist. Frankly, it is offensive to suggest that we can, Ralph, and if you offend me again, I shall have to punish you."

Admonished thus, Ralph's ears sag, meekly, and he decides he will keep quiet rather than risk punishment by speaking up again.

"But what about the inventors?" asks Charlie. "Why did you take their posters down? And Mayor Blinkin ended slavery. Were they all pred supremacists, too?"

The schoolmaster glares at the young coyote. "In the future, Charlie, do not speak unless called upon. In answer to your question, yes, Mayor Blinkin was a specist, and the inventors probably were too. At the very least they were part of the pred culture that uses science and technology to enforce pred supremacy. You see, class, pred culture created so-called *science* and the notion that there is *objective knowledge* as a means to dominate prey. Pred supremacists use science and objectivity as justification for disregarding prey ways of knowing that reach different conclusions."

Puzzled looks appear on the children's faces. Floppy finally raises his paw. "Yes, Floppy," says Dr. Greenbitter, smiling pleasantly. "I have been waiting to hear from you, after all the good things Mr. Hoofman had to say about you."

"Gee, thanks, ma'am," Floppy says, bashfully. "Mr. Hoofman taught us that animal freedom depends on knowledge and that knowledge is why all animals are now free. Was Mr. Hoofman wrong?"

"Ah, but what is knowledge, Floppy? Who has the right to say what counts as knowledge and what does not? Whom does so-called knowledge really serve? Ask yourself: what kind of species is the richest animal in town, and what kind has every mayor before Mayor Middleton been? Preds, Floppy, all preds, and that is not by accident; that is pred supremacy at work. Pred knowledge serves pred interests."

"So... Mr. Luckson... has more freedom... because he's a pred and not because he has more knowledge?" Floppy implores, his blue eyes sparkling.

"Exactly. Mr. Luckson and the other preds of Animal Town benefit from pred supremacy, and that is why some animals have more freedom than others. Knowledge has nothing to do with it. Mr. Hoofman was wrong to say that it does. It seems he internalized pred culture, as many prey of his generation have done."

Dr. Greenbitter speaks with conviction. Her voice falters with emotion, and the hair on the scruff of her neck bristles under her sweater collar. She gathers herself and addresses one of the pred paws that remains in the air, "Yes, Sylvester?"

"Well *I'm* not a pred supremacist, or a specist, or anything like that, and *my* family is not rich like the Lucksons, and I don't think I have more freedom than the prey either," declares the grey wolf pup.

"Ah, yes. I was expecting this," replies Dr. Greenbitter. "Class, this is called '*pred fragility*.' Whenever preds are confronted with pred supremacy, they instinctively deny that it benefits them and often that it even exists. They are so unused to having their dominance challenged that they are hypersensitive to perceived attacks."

As she speaks these words, Dr. Greenbitter walks down the center aisle, passes the two prey rows, and looks up and down the two pred rows, meaningfully. Then she stops and stares directly at the young wolf. "Now listen closely, Sylvester, and the rest of you preds as well. You may not think you are a specist, but you nevertheless have a *subconscious prejudice* against prey that causes you to discriminate against us without even knowing it. The only way for you or any pred to overcome your inherent specism is to acknowledge constantly your subconscious prejudice and work continuously to dismantle pred supremacy. If you are not anti-specist, then you are specist. You are either a prey ally or an enemy. There is no grey area.

"Furthermore, even if you are not a pred supremacist, you and all preds bear the guilt of your ancestors' specism and benefit from pred supremacy to this day. You are born with *pred privilege*, and it will never go away until pred supremacy has been reversed."

The preds shift in their seats, uncomfortably.

"So, let us begin the dismantling work right here in this classroom: I want all the preds to repeat after me: *even if I am not a pred supremacist, I benefit from pred supremacy.*"

The preds mutter softly in response, "Even if I am not a pred supremacist, I benefit from pred supremacy."

"Louder, preds. Keep in mind that I am grading you on class participation. Again."

"Even if I am not a pred supremacist, I benefit from pred supremacy," comes the response, more emphatic this time.

"Again!" Dr. Greenbitter commands, in her squeaky voice.

"Even if I am not a pred supremacist, I benefit from pred supremacy!" shout the pred children, rattling the windows and involuntarily bearing their fangs. Dr. Greenbitter and several of the prey children startle at the sight of pointy white teeth.

The young gopher smoothes down her bristling fur and adjusts her frames on her nose. "That is a good start. Thank you," she says. "Class, we shall now break for recess."

The children slowly rise from their seats and move toward the door in silence. The preds do so with their eyes downcast and their tails between their legs.

CHAPTER 5

"*Honk, honk!*" That night, a Canada goose soars over Animal Town, emitting an occasional honk from his narrow beak. With his majestic black hood, long neck, and broad wingspan, he is a sight to behold, in the prime of his feathered life. It is Avery, the town newspaper owner, reporter, and editor. Avery studied journalism at Animal Town University and took over the daily paper, The Animal Times, not long after graduating. He is making his nightly rounds flying high above Animal Town, searching out news with his piercing black eyes. The paper will be printed overnight, and Avery needs a story.

After tracing a wide circle over the town, seeing nothing newsworthy, Avery swoops down from the sky and alights in front of Animal Town Social Club. The club is situated adjacent to Animal Town's leading institutions: Town Hall and Courthouse, the Mayor's Residence, and ATU. At the center of the ornate buildings is the neatly landscaped Town Square, populated with statues of eminent animals from the town's past, including several whose portraits were recently removed from Luckson All

Animal School. Fronting the square, the exclusive club counts the town's leading animals among its members. As is his custom, Avery has stopped to check on events among the elite, for they often have news for him.

At the club entrance, he displays his press credential to the dooranimal. The bear unhesitatingly waves him into the club.

Inside, Avery finds many of the town's most prominent residents, as well as their lackeys. To the right, seated around the fireplace on sumptuous, high-backed chairs, are the Lucksons, Camilla the sheep, and Judge Cavendish, the aged mountain lion who decides on matter of law for Animal Town. The four animals sip scotch in hushed conversation. By the bar, the town doctor chats up one of the two jill weasels who previously entertained the Junior Luckson. Ahead, Avery spots Mayor Middleton, conversing pleasantly with a cluster of animals who hang on his every word. "Oh, I agree, Mr. Mayor," Avery overhears an eagle say. "How right you are." A wise and worldly animal, Mayor Middleton is respected and admired by nearly all the townsanimals.

Hoping for a newsworthy quote from the mayor, Avery waddles toward the group. As he does so, the tall, proud pronghorn recognizes and turns to greet him. "Well hullo, Avery. What news in Animal Town today?" As usual, the mayor is looking square and sharp in an understated navy suit and light blue necktie.

"Unfortunately, there's not much to report, Mayor

Middleton, aside from a new schoolmaster taking over at Luckson All Animal School. Incidentally, might I ask you a question or two on the record?"

"Why certainly, Avery, I always have time for you. A free and fair press is one of the pillars of democracy, as I never tire of pointing out. And I know I can count on you to be fair."

"You can, Sir. The Times prides itself on accuracy and objectivity," the goose says, pulling a small audio recorder from under his wing.

"Mayor Middleton," he begins, "your second and final term is almost at an end. You will preside over your last town meeting tomorrow night. Looking back on your time as mayor, how would you describe your legacy?"

"Glad you asked that, Ave," says the mayor in his sonorous, formal voice. "Things have never been better in Animal Town. The economy has grown consistently during my mayoralty and is larger than ever. Fewer animals of every species are out of work, inequality between preds and prey is lower than ever, and more animals have access to health care than any time in animal memory. Meanwhile, the crime rate has steadily decreased during my mayoralty, and animal has not killed animal for generations. I dare say harmony reigns in Animal Town. Though I am not too concerned about my legacy, I hope animals of all species enjoyed peaceful, prosperous lives during my time as mayor."

"Thank you, Mr. Mayor," responds Avery. "I can attest that I've had less and less crime to report since I took over the paper—probably why I've been selling fewer and fewer papers—but, if I may: it is true that unemployment is at a historic low, though it is also true that wages have remained stagnant for a generation. As The Times has reported, many working animals earn less than their parents did at the same age, but the cost of housing, health care, and other necessities has increased. Further, perhaps you saw our special report on inequality last month? It pointed out that, while inequality between preds and prey has decreased, as you say, inequality between the rich and everyone else is steadily *increasing*. Today the richest few animals own more than all other animals combined. How do you respond to the contention that your mayoralty has mostly benefited a small number of wealthy animals? Some of those animals, like the Lucksons, are in this very room; I should point out."

Mayor Middleton furrows his brow. "Let me be clear," he says. "Some inequality is to be expected, and it is not always a bad thing. You mentioned Mr. Luckson. It is true that he is a wealthy animal, indeed the wealthiest in town. But he donated part of that wealth to build the new schoolhouse, you may recall, and that benefits every animal in town. Does it not?"

"Well said, Mr. Mayor," the eagle needlessly adds.

"Now, if you will excuse me, Ave, I really must be going. I still have to put the finishing touches on my parting remarks for tomorrow's town meeting." The mayor speaks with finality. Though he means what he says about the importance of the press, one thing he will not miss after stepping down as mayor is answering Avery's probing questions. He takes his leave of the animals surrounding him, offering a hearty hoofshake to each. Then he trots out the door of the social club.

At the other side of the room, around the fireplace, two weasels and a sheep are discussing business, as a mountain lion listens intently.

"Revenues are up three percent this lunar cycle." Resting one paw on his gold-handled cane, Mr. Luckson takes a sip of his scotch before continuing. "Most of that comes from Camilla's diligent work collecting from the preds—well done, Camilla. Revenue from prey, however, has been flat for some time, *Junior*."

"Thank you, Mr. Luckson," Camilla responds. "I am just doing what you've taught me."

"You're just lucky that preds are better at paying their rent!" snipes Junior. "The prey are full of excuses. If I got to collect from the easy preds, I would put little Camilla to shame, Daddy. Believe me!"

"I'm happy to switch, *Junior*, and I will still bring in more rocks than you!"

"Don't call me Junior! It's *Mr.* Luckson to you!" comes the rejoinder.

"That's enough, both of you," injects Mr. Luckson Sr.

"We mustn't make a scene in front of the honored judge."

Judge Cavendish's large belly squeezes against his three-piece suit when he leans forward to say, "Never mind me, old chap. I like being privy to inside information. That's how a good politician keeps abreast of events. Speaking of events," he says, pausing to flick ash from his cigar before replacing it in his mouth, "you may recall that I am up for reelection next winter. What with your increased revenues, it seems you could afford to donate to my, er, political fund."

"Do you hear that?" says Mr. Luckson, glancing toward his son and employee. "Typical politician, always with his paw out!"

As the four animals converse, Avery works the room. He speaks to several leading animals but fails to learn anything newsworthy. He hears idle speculation regarding who might replace Mr. Middleton as mayor, but, as no candidates have yet been nominated, he will not deign to publish such gossip. It is beneath his lofty journalistic standards.

All the same, Avery is worried. If he does not find a better story by night's end, he will have no choice but to run a front-page article about Dr. Greenbitter taking over as schoolmaster. *Hardly a story to make animals run to buy a paper*, he thinks.

In the hope of discovering late-breaking news before printing tomorrow's papers, Avery decides to make one more flight over Animal Town. Soon he is high in the air once more.

CHAPTER 6

Earlier that evening, in a humbler part of Animal Town, Floppy went straight home from school. After Dr. Greenbitter's lecture Charlie was in no mood for pawball, and, at any rate, Floppy had to hurry home to watch over his little brothers and prepare the family dinner. The two friends spoke nary a word to one another after the final bell.

Upon reaching his den, Floppy spends several hours gently rocking his baby brothers in their crib by the fireplace. His sister Lepu plays quietly in the next room. As the innocents sleep, Floppy gazes absently into the licking flames of the low fire, tending conflicting ideas in his mind's soil. One thought that grows is concern for his friend, Charlie, and his other pred classmates. He feels their humiliation at being made to accuse themselves in front of the class. They have never treated him badly because of his species, and he does not feel he is a victim of pred supremacy. *After all, I often get the best grade in class*, he thinks. Nevertheless, he is worried that Dr. Greenbitter's teachings might come between him and his friend. At the same time, the seedling of another idea begins to grow in a new direction. Floppy is gratified Dr.

Greenbitter confirmed his suspicion that Mr. Luckson has more freedom than other animals. He is ready to accept her explanation that this is because he has pred privilege, for he can readily identify well-known preds, like Mr. Luckson and previous mayors, who appear to have more freedom than him and his family.

Floppy is so lost in his field of thought that he forgets to prepare dinner by the time his parents finally return from the Luckson Shiny Rock Mine, late in the evening.

The den's crooked door swings open, and two jackrabbits trudge in, covered in rock dust. Jolted from his reverie, Floppy rushes to embrace his parents.

"Hiya, Dad. Hiya, Mom," he says. After exchanging greetings with their children, and doffing their filthy overalls, his parents notice that dinner has not been prepared. They question Floppy about its absence.

"Gee, I'm sorry," Floppy says, rushing to the pantry in search of food. "I guess I was daydreaming." Opening the pantry door, he sees a variety of bags and sacks slumping limply in all directions. They had once held fruit, grain, and vegetables, but now all are empty—except for one, that is, which contains a single carrot. To afford double rent next month, his parents have had to ration their food still more stringently, and this means that tonight there is not enough to go around. Floppy rifles the bags hastily and extracts the lone carrot. Closing the pantry door behind him, he holds it out to his parents, without looking them in the eyes.

"Is that all there is?" his mother asks. "Yes, I suppose it is. Well, chop it up and give it to the kits please, Floppy. The rest of us will have to be content with hot water and lemon tonight."

Floppy has already begun cutting up the carrot into little pieces suitable for kits. Without looking up, he says, meekly, "We're out of lemons."

Hearing this, Floppy's father becomes irate. "Not even Lemons! Fire it all! We work at that mine for fourteen hours a day and we still can't afford lemons? Well, we *could* afford them if we didn't have to save every shiny rock to pay that greedy old weasel!" Jack is practically shouting. This frightens his family, as he rarely raises his voice. The infant twins begin to cry.

"Jack, please. Don't lose your temper in front of the kids. I can pick up a lemon and a few other things after work tomorrow. We'll manage." Lil attempts to mollify him.

"I'm serious, Lil. I have half a mind to march over to Luckson's mansion and tell him where to stick his shiny rocks!"

Jack's anger is uncharacteristic. He is a measured, rational rabbit, in general, and he is typically soft-spoken and obsequious toward his employer. But seeing his family go hungry stirs baser instincts. The thought of Mr. Luckson living in luxury while his family starves triggers strong emotions, deep in his hare brain, and makes rational thought impossible. Jack's emotional outburst sweeps up his son, Floppy, who idolizes his father and has recently been given reason to resent Mr. Luckson in his own right.

Attempting to be supportive and imitating his father's outrage, Floppy chimes in, "Yeah! He's a pred supremacist! He doesn't deserve to be rich just because he's a pred!"

"What's that about pred supremacist, Floppy? Where did you hear that word?" asks Jack, startled at his son's speech.

"I learned it in school today. Our new schoolmaster, Dr. Greenbitter, says that Mr. Luckson and the other preds have more freedom because of pred supremacy and specism."

"That's silly talk," injects his mother, with a doubtful look on her face. "All animals are equally free in Animal Town. Mr. Luckson is rich because he owns everything, not because he's a pred."

"But Dr. Greenbitter says that pred culture is defined by greed and specism and that whenever preds like Mr. Luckson have more power, it is because of, because of sis-systemic specism."

"That's enough, Floppy," chides Lil. "Fill a big glass of water for you and your sister, and both of you go to bed. You won't be hungry when you're asleep. Your father and I will bring home food for dinner tomorrow. Not to worry."

"Yes, off to bed, both of you," adds Jack, absentmindedly. He has calmed somewhat, but his son's words have stirred his thoughts. As his two oldest children close the door to their room, obeying their parents' command, he flops down in a chair and begins to think.

Exhausted by the long day at the mine, Lil wants no more of the argument and busies herself feeding the carrot pieces to her young sons. Once they are fed, she tucks them in, puts another piece of wood on the fire, and climbs to bed in the loft above the crib.

"Don't stay up too late," she calls to her husband.

Jack does not reply.

An hour after he is sure everyone in his family is asleep, Jack slips out the crooked den door. A sliver of waxing crescent moon casts a pale light upon the winter night into which he steps. He hops hastily in the direction of Animal Town Lake.

A goose soars overhead, unnoticed.

Jack soon reaches his destination. On a high bluff overlooking the lake, a forty-room mansion spreads two wings before him, divided by the central pillars and pediment. Three-story columns draw his eyes upward until they fix on Mr. Luckson Sr.'s bedroom window at the center of the structure. The garish, pastel peach bricks appear gray in the moonlight. From pictures Jack knows the famed residence well, as do all the citizens of Animal Town, but this is his first time on the grounds.

Panting softly and emitting tiny puffs of breath into the frigid air, Jack is careful to move silently. Officer Furman might be patrolling nearby. He skirts the edge of the grounds until he spots his adventure's aim: a long glass greenhouse where Mr. Luckson's gardener grows flowers and vegetables for his master's table all year-round. The panes are foggy with condensation from the heat within.

Jack approaches stealthily, his eyes darting about him and his ears at attention. His heart throbs. He is alone, save for the goose gliding unbeknownst overhead, watching expectantly. He reaches the greenhouse door and is surprised to find it unlocked. This boosts his confidence. *Stupid weasel*, he thinks as he pushes it ajar and steps in.

His nose is met by a fragrant waft of flower pollen which sneaks out the door behind him. Dimly, his eyes see the silhouette of a magnificent garden, full bloom in the dead of winter. His heart jumps and his stomach rumbles expectantly. *There's enough to feed half the town*, Jack tells himself. *Mr. Luckson won't even notice what's gone.*

Quietly, he gathers a dozen carrots, a few potatoes, and some pawfuls of peapods, stuffing them into his satchel. He takes care to fill in the dirt from whence he extracted the tubers and to otherwise cover the evidence of his theft. Sold at market, the vegetables' value is less than five grams of shiny rocks. He begins to relax and prepares to return home, thinking the job was so easy he might try it again next month.

Meanwhile, an unexpected fragrance reaches the sensitive nose of a black bear, lumbering along the lakeshore on the opposite side of Luckson Manor. *Lilies*, Furman says to himself. *I'm sure of it.* With his nose jutting into the air and his nostrils flaring wide, the bear traces the scent back to its source. He reaches the greenhouse just as Jack is closing the door behind him.

"Halt!" shouts Furman.

Jack startles, involuntarily jumping high in the air, straight up and into a moonbeam. His terrified face is bathed in pale light, and Furman recognizes the jackrabbit from their encounter a few days before.

"It's you!" the bear growls. His glands pump adrenaline, and the thick black fur on his back bristles automatically. He cannot help the spontaneous response. Given the rarity of crime in Animal Town, Furman is unpracticed at apprehending perpetrators.

Stricken with fear, Jack lands awkwardly. He pushes off with his muscular hind legs once more, attempting to flee. Normally a jackrabbit is far more agile than a black bear, but, weighed down by the illicit satchel, Jack is at a disadvantage.

"I said halt!" Furman lunges at the hungry, thieving

hare, his paw outstretched in his path. Jack trips over the bear's claws, falling on his side and spilling the contents of the satchel over the frosty grass. He scrambles to gather the produce.

Instinctively, the bear pounces, pinning the hare to the ground, his broad paws pressed against Jack's neck.

A dull snap propagates through the cold.

The black bear bellows deeply, throwing back his head and roaring with such ferocity that the goose flying overhead nearly falls out of the sky with fright. The force of his roar rattles the panes of the glass greenhouse. Lights appear in the mansion windows as the Lucksons rouse from their comfortable sleep.

"You're under arrest!" says Furman, releasing Jack's neck and reaching for his paw-cuffs. "What have you got to say for yourself?"

Jack lies limp, his head angled unnaturally from his body, his eyes glossy. For the first time in living memory, animal has killed animal.

Slowly realizing what he has done, Officer Furman drops the paw-cuffs and staggers back several paces, until his back is against the greenhouse wall. He doubles over and vomits. Wiping his mouth with the back of his paw, he slumps to the ground, dazed and unmoving but for the heaving of his chest.

Avery swoops down and lands by the corpse. He

scribbles notes hastily and snaps pictures. The Lucksons, too, are soon on the scene. They quickly recover from their initial shock and assure Furman he has done no more than his duty, for which he will be handsomely rewarded. They call Judge Cavendish, who arrives promptly. After he questions Furman and Avery, the judge releases the stunned bear into the Lucksons' custody, pending his decision whether he is guilty of a crime, which he will render at the town meeting the following night. The stiffening jackrabbit carcass is hauled off to the morgue, unceremoniously.

Once the commotion is over, Avery flies to The Animal Times office, shaking with excitement. He furiously bangs out a new front-page article for the morning's paper, relegating Dr. Greenbitter to page two. The headline reads, in all capital letters, *PREDATOR KILLS PREY!*

It is the first edition to sell out in years.

CHAPTER 7

The evening after the event, also for the first time in years, Animal Town Hall and Courthouse is packed to the rafters an hour before the monthly meeting begins. Birds and mammals, predators and prey squeeze tightly together on long wooden benches. Others stand close on the balcony overlooking the main hall, where the air soon becomes sticky from wafting body heat. All have read The Animal Times and are there to learn what will result from the first unnatural animal death since before they were born, or hatched.

As ever, prominent animals occupy the front rows. Behind the Lucksons, Camilla, and Furman are Judge Cavendish, Avery, and Mr. Hoofman. Dr. Greenbitter, school board members, and ATU faculty occupy the next row. Laboring animals fill in the remaining benches and balcony above. Customarily, predators and prey sit intermixed at town meetings, but on this day they have self-segregated. To the left of the center aisle are bison, deer, pronghorn, sheep, gophers, jackrabbits, geese, and pheasants—the prey of Animal Town. Conspicuous among the prey is Jack's widow, Lil, clad in black with her ears drooping pathetically at her sides. Her fatherless kits and the other children of Animal Town are at home, as town meetings are for grown animals only. To the right of the center aisle are wolves, coyotes, foxes, mountain lions, bears, weasels, and eagles—the preds of Animal Town. Inconspicuous among the preds, standing at the far right of the balcony and barely visible in the shadows, is Mr. Scratch. His jaw is set and his eyes gleam.

After some minutes of expectant waiting, the hot, murmuring crowd falls silent. Mayor Middleton appears at the entrance. He walks the aisle between them and mounts the platform at the front of the hall, one hoof at a time. The whiskers on his cheeks have begun to gray.

He stands behind an ancient wooden podium, used since the early days of Animal Town, where all his mayoral predecessors once stood to address the citizenry. Silent for several seconds, he looks about the room into the faces of the gathered animals. An astute observer could just see disappointment flash across his face when he notices that preds and prey are sitting separately. Through his nostrils, he emits an inaudible sigh, and then he opens his mouth to speak.

"My fellow animals," he begins, in his lofty tenor voice. "I had hoped that my farewell address would mark a happy moment in our town's history—a moment to look back with satisfaction upon years of steady progress and to look forward with confident expectation of still better years to come. Alas, events have intervened. And though I remain satisfied with our progress and confident in our future, I would be remiss if I did not comment on the incident last night, which no doubt occupies our minds today."

Mayor Middleton pauses while his preamble sinks in. Then he continues, "The unthinkable has happened: animal has killed animal. A wife has been unnaturally deprived of her husband and children of their father. Let us keep this grieving jackrabbit family foremost in our minds, for it is they who most need our compassion and support at this difficult time. But, while we are right to give them our attention, let us not forget that there is another victim in this tragedy, one whose life is likewise forever altered. I am speaking of Officer Furman. Just as Jack, may he rest in peace, did what he believed necessary to feed his family, Officer Furman did what he believed necessary to uphold the law. We must observe the principle of charity and assume neither Jack nor Officer Furman acted with mal intent."

A few low grumbles rise from the left, prey side of the hall. Mayor Middleton tactfully ignores them.

"Let me be clear, it is not my position to opine on the legality of either of their actions. We are fortunate to live in a town governed by the rule of law, and the law says the determination of Jack and Officer Furman's guilt or innocence must fall to Judge Cavendish. I have neither comment nor influence on the Judge's decision, which he will render before you here tonight.

"I only urge you to calmly and rationally consider both sides of the case from the objective perspective of the law.

Recall that the statue of Lady Justice which stands in front of this hall wears a blindfold for good reason. For the law takes no heed of an animal's species—whether bird or mammal, predator or prey—but, rather, Lady Justice impartially weighs the facts in her scales and dispenses justice with her sword without regard to the identities of the litigants. This is what equal justice under law requires, and I urge you to likewise view the matter from this perspective.

"Now, you may be predisposed to view the matter otherwise; I know. You might be biased by whether you have a hoof or a claw, a beak or a paw, and be led to judge the matter, 'as a predator...' or 'as a prey...' rather than *as a citizen*. Indeed, even as we speak, some are preparing to divide us, the spin masters and myth peddlers who embrace the politics of species before citizenship. They will tell us that Jack and Officer Furman must be judged not as individuals but instead as representatives of all prey or all predators. They will say the law must recognize collective guilt and collective innocence, that what matters is not what we do but what we *are*. Well, I say to them tonight, there is not a bird town and a mammal town—there is an *Animal* Town. There is not a prey town and a predator town—there is an *Animal* Town. Though we are not equal in outward form, we are yet equal in inner worth and political rights. We are all part of this great project together, and we will not be divided.

"Because I know and endorse these truths, I can still say to you with satisfaction that, despite this tragedy, things have never been better in Animal Town. I can say with confidence that, if we stay the course, this will remain true tomorrow, and the day after that, and the day after that, for as long and we remember that all animals are brothers and sisters and not members of warring species."

Mayor Middleton's words reverberate through the hushed hall. He was expecting applause at the last line, but it fails to materialize. He sighs again, and his usually erect posture slumps somewhat.

Speaking softer now, the pronghorn closes. "My time as mayor is at an end, and I am leaving Animal Town on the morrow. As is our custom, my last official act is to appoint a worthy citizen to chair next month's town meeting, at which candidates to replace me as mayor will be nominated. For this role, I select Mr. Hoofman and thus discharge my duty as your mayor. Goodbye, and may goodness prevail in Animal Town." Mr. Middleton steps down from the platform and exits the hall, never to be seen again.

Moments later, Judge Cavendish takes his place at the podium. Now it is his turn to speak, and the hush that met the noble pronghorn's speech remains in place as the black-robed mountain lion begins to dispense justice.

"I will be brief," says the fat old judge, "as the case before me is a simple one. Here are the facts: Jack, the deceased rabbit, attempted to steal from Mr. Luckson Sr. Officer Furman caught him in the act while patrolling near the Luckson residence. Jack attempted to flee the scene with stolen property. Officer Furman sought to apprehend Jack. In the process, Jack was killed. Cause of death was a broken neck."

Lil groans audibly. The surrounding prey comfort her.

Judge Cavendish continues, in his brusque tone, "My verdict is as follows: Officer Furman used appropriate force in his apprehension of the suspect, and he is found innocent of any crime. Further, he is commended for his law enforcement action and hereby awarded the Distinguished Service Medal."

Many of the assembled animals gasp audibly. Confusion reigns as Lil swoons and falls into her prey companions' arms. Officer Furman exhales heavily and grins. The Lucksons slap him on the back and offer their congratulations. Dr. Greenbitter scowls in anger, and Mr. Scratch's yellow eyes sparkle with delight. Lil is just returning to her senses when Judge Cavendish continues.

"As for the rabbit, Jack, upon review of the evidence and Officer Furman's testimony, he is found guilty of larceny and trespassing. I posthumously convict him of these crimes. Further, given that he died committing criminal acts, his next of kin are denied benefits or restitution from the town. The matter is settled." Pronouncing thus, Judge Cavendish pounds his gavel against its block, sending a sharp crack echoing through the courtroom.

Lil faints a second time.

"There is *pred justice* for you!" shouts Dr. Greenbitter, trembling with feeling. Mr. Scratch cackles with glee. Contrasting emotions take hold of the two sides of the hall.

Judge Cavendish pounds his gavel again, sending ripples through his gelatinous arm, all the way up to his double chin. "Order in my courtroom!" he demands, his chin wobbling with the force of his speech. "Order or I will hold you in contempt of court! I will not stand for any talk of *pred justice*. It insults the dignity of my office and the authority the town has vested in me. Need I remind you? The law is blind to species, but the right to property is absolute and must be upheld. It is *this* right Jack sought to undermine through his cowardly theft and *this* right Officer Furman sought to uphold through his heroic service."

"Silly rabbit got what he had coming! Serves him right!" calls Mr. Scratch.

Dr. Greenbitter whips her head around to glare at the fox above her. Then she turns back to the ATU faculty and school board members seated around her. Looking in their faces and rhythmically shaking her clenched paws, she begins chanting, "Prey lives matter! Prey lives matter!" Several of her companions join the chorus, drowning out other prey voices. Some of the preds growl and gnash their teeth in response.

"Do you hear that my good preds?" shouts Mr. Scratch, leaning over the balcony. "The prey have no respect for the law! Come see me at the Great Predator Temple if you want to do something about it!"

Through the din, Judge Cavendish calls Officer Furman to the platform and pleads with him to restore order. Already angry at the prey behavior, the bear inhales deeply, preparing to roar the courtroom into stunned silence. Just as he is about to let loose, he feels a slight tug of his left paw. With breath still filing his barrel chest, he looks down and sees Lil staring up at him, her face fur streaked with tears. In her pleading expression, Furman reads "No more, please. No more." Touched by pity for the rabbit he widowed, the burly bear exhales silently, and the rage rising within him subsides.

He raises his arms high in the air and says, evenly, "Quiet please."

The sight of the massive black bear, a known animal killer, towering above them prompts the animals to gradually fall silent once again.

Furman lowers his arms. "Lil has something to say."

All eyes fix on the sad little jackrabbit, clad in black.

"My Jack is gone," she says with quiet conviction. "That is enough. I don't want any more grief to come from his death. My children are hungry, scared, and alone. I am going home to be with them. Please go home to be with your own families, and I hope you never have to face the grief that we must."

After speaking these words, Lil descends from the platform and hops silently down the center aisle and through the large double doors at front of the hall. Her dignified plea calms the fervor that had quickly caught up to the animals. Soon others file out behind her, some talking in low voices.

As the meeting breaks up and the animals make for their homes, Avery is seen interviewing Dr. Greenbitter. The goose and gopher stand under the sword of the Lady Justice statue, in close conversation.

CHAPTER 8

Mr. Luckson is pleased with himself. He sits at his marble countertop, eats a hearty breakfast—too much food for one weasel, really—and reads The Animal Times' account of the trial. The front-page headline reads, *Pred Justice?*

Just look at that headline, he thinks to himself. *That's the most beautiful headline I have ever seen.* What's more, Dr. Greenbitter has written an editorial calling it an *outrage* that Officer Furman was awarded a medal for killing Jack. *This is not animal justice. This is systemic specism at work,* she writes.

"It's almost too good to be true," Mr. Luckson says aloud when he reads the line. "That was the best campaign donation I ever made."

Mr. Luckson refers to the fifty kilos of shiny rocks that he contributed to Judge Cavendish's "political fund" on the night of the fateful event. That night, after Avery left the scene, Judge Cavendish lingered to discuss matters with the Lucksons. Careful not to suggest an explicit *quid pro quo,* the judge had simply remarked that it would be unfortunate if Jack's actions inspired other poor animals to likewise take matters into their own paws. "That could be trouble for wealthy animals like yourselves," the lion said nonchalantly. "Incidentally, you will no doubt recall that I am up for reelection next year." Taking the hint, Mr. Luckson then invited the judge to join him and Junior inside their home while Furman remained on guard outside. Some minutes later, the judge emerged from Luckson Manor carrying a canvas bag, laden with shiny rocks.

When he handed the bag over to the judge, Mr. Luckson had said, with a wink and a nod, "Please accept a political contribution from the Luckson Family Corporation, anonymously of course. I can think of no better animal to ensure that property is protected and order is maintained in our town." Such is the manner in which politics are conducted in Animal Town.

Now the verdict is in, and Mr. Luckson believes the danger has passed. Judge Cavendish has sent a strong message to the poor of animal town that thievery, even to feed a hungry family, will not be tolerated. Moreover, Mr. Luckson sees an opportunity in the division between preds and prey that the incident has precipitated. Over the ensuing days, he sets out to exploit this division to his advantage.

Mr. Luckson first invites the new schoolmaster, Dr.

Greenbitter, to pay him a visit. His butler delivers a card to her at the schoolhouse, wherein it is written, *Please honor me with your presence at Luckson Manor tomorrow evening. I wish to make the acquaintance of the master of the school which bears my name. Sincerely, Lyle Luckson Sr.*

Though she is initially wary of visiting the site where a fellow prey was recently killed, the invitation is too enticing for Dr. Greenbitter to reject. *Here is my chance to make an ally of the richest animal in town*, she thinks when she arrives at the estate on the appointed date.

The young gopher stands in the portico, straightening her frames and flattening her rumpled sweater. The large oak door swings open. "Welcome to Luckson Manor, Dr. Greenbitter," drawls the butler, making a sweeping motion with his arm. "Won't you come in?" Dressed in starched servant's livery, the bison appears an anachronism to the schoolmaster's eyes.

"Thank you," she says, crossing the threshold.

The butler continues, formally, "Mr. Luckson is eager to make your acquaintance, madam. If it pleases you to turn left at the top of the staircase, you shall find him in the west wing."

The golden gopher mounts the red-carpeted stairs, following the butler's directions, and soon finds herself face-to-face with the old weasel whose ancestors once hunted her ancestors.

"Aha! There you are, Ms. Greenbitter! I am so pleased that you could make it. Did you have any trouble finding the place?" Mr. Luckson beams warmly and embraces Dr. Greenbitter.

"No, no. Of course not. I know the address well. It is an honor to meet you, sir," Dr. Greenbitter responds.

They sit and begin to talk. In the following minutes, the crafty weasel ingratiates himself with the young gopher through deft conversation. He inquires about her past, how she finds All Animal School and its pupils, and about her studies at ATU. He listens intently, looks into her eyes, and repeats her name often, seeming to hang upon her every word. When she reports that she has, in fact, earned a doctorate in prey studies, he apologizes profusely for not referring to her by her proper title. "How terribly foolish of me. It won't happen again," he promises. "Yours is a most essential field of study, and your students are lucky to have you as their schoolmaster," he gushes. For her part, Dr. Greenbitter is flattered to be fawned over by so eminent an animal as Mr. Luckson. She is glad she accepted his invitation.

After several minutes, sensing his quarry sufficiently prepared, Mr. Luckson strikes. "By the way," he says, "I happened to read your editorial in The Animal Times recently. I was quite impressed, and I must say it has caused me to rethink a few things."

"Is that so?" asks Dr. Greenbitter, with interest.

"Yes, indeed. You make a strong case that Officer Furman's acquittal and Jack's conviction are the result of systemic specism in Animal Town's justice system. Of course, I feel terrible that the incident happened on my property. I would have gladly given Jack the food he attempted to steal, but, alas, Officer Furman was too zealous in carrying out his duty."

"That's just it," says the gopher, growing animated. "Officer Furman's duty, whether he knows it or not, is to enforce pred interests."

"So you say, and I am inclined to agree with you," responds Mr. Luckson, "for you have opened my eyes to the truth: Animal Town is governed by pred justice, but it deserves animal justice."

"Exactly!" Dr. Greenbitter enthuses. "If only all preds were as honest as you, we could dismantle pred supremacy in no time!"

"It cannot happen soon enough if you ask me," says the weasel. "In fact, that is why I asked you here tonight. You see, since reading your article, I have begun to feel guilty about being a predator, not only because of the pred privilege from which I benefit, but also for the crimes of my ancestors. I feel ashamed that my pred forebears once conquered and enslaved innocent prey. Why, the first pred to exploit prey in this part of the world was a weasel. I might even be his descendent, stained forever by his heinous crimes against the noble natives." So earnestly does Mr. Luckson intone these words that his voice trembles.

"I fear you may be right," says Dr. Greenbitter, matching his solemnity.

"That's why I feel compelled to make a donation to your school, if you will deign to accept it. I simply must clear my bad conscience of this pred guilt by supporting your effort to expose children to pred supremacy. Of course, the donation must be anonymous. Given the current inter-species tension, it might look bad if it were known to come from a pred. Moreover, I want the attention to be on prey issues, not myself. In fact, if you'll agree, I'd like to see the school renamed for a more worthy animal. I thought perhaps the great Marcus Prince would be appropriate."

At the mention of a donation, Dr. Greenbitters eyes widen. "That's wonderful! How generous of you, Mr. Luckson! Thank you so much!"

Not at all. It really is the least I can do. It's only a matter of, let's say, twenty-five kilos of shiny rocks for the school… and perhaps another twenty-five kilos for the schoolmaster herself? I know it has been several years since your adjacent living quarters have been updated, and no one is more deserving than you, Dr. Greenbitter." As he speaks, Mr. Luckson smiles widely, winks, and nods.

Upon hearing the large sum she is to receive, Dr. Greenbitter nearly falls out of her chair. "You really are too kind, sir," she exclaims. "What a wonderful surprise.

Thank you. Thank you very much!"

"Call it amends made long overdue. Just continue to speak out *against* pred supremacy and *for* animal justice, and I will consider it a wise investment. What do you think of the name change, by the way?"

"Oh, I agree Marcus Prince is appropriate. I shall see to it right away."

"That settles it then," says the weasel. "I really am so glad we met this evening; my conscience feels clearer already." He extends his paw and the gopher shakes it heartily.

The day after this meeting, Mr. Luckson's butler could be seen dropping off a heavily laden canvas bag at the schoolhouse. When he does so, Dr. Greenbitter is busy erecting a sign bearing the school's new name.

Mr. Luckson's next target is Mr. Scratch, leader of the Great Predator Temple of Animal Town. Though he has not had occasion to meet the eccentric canid, he is old enough to remember the rumors of the fiery sermons he once delivered; talk was he preached to preds only. His interest in Mr. Scratch was further piqued by the fox's recent outbursts in court. Thus, seeking to determine if the aged fox might serve his purposes, the day after his meeting with Dr. Greenbitter, Mr. Luckson dispatches his butler with a similar invitation to Mr. Scratch.

The appointed date of their meeting soon arrives. The interview takes place in the parlor of Luckson Manor. Wood paneling and portraits of Luckson ancestors cover the walls, the most prominent of which is the family fortune's founder, he who had his burrow at the river rapids. A crystal chandelier augments the glow of the fireplace, which burns opposite a wide balcony overlooking Animal Town Lake. The two preds are seated in front of the fire. The aged fox wears a dingy black frock coat, patched at the elbows. His yellow eyes are shifty and inquisitive of his unaccustomed surroundings, his ears alert. The weasel wears a custom made, continental suit in a gingham pattern. He is calm and his posture inviting.

"Our meeting is long overdue," begins Mr. Luckson, "and the fault is entirely my own. It seems my work is never done, and I am left with too little time for socializing."

"I don't much care for socializing myself, not with most animals anyhow."

"Really? What do you mean by that?"

"I mean an animal is better off alone and righteous than popular and damned." The fox's speech is clipped and harsh.

"Interestingly put. Care to elaborate?" is the weasel's polite rejoinder.

"The animals in this town have been corrupted. The

pred culture that made Animal Town great is under attack, species mingle indiscriminately, and animals have lost faith in the Great Pred Father. In a time like this, a decent pred finds few friends. Just look at that slippery gopher they have put in charge of the school, writing about pred justice and chanting in court. Did you know that she had the gall to change its name to Marcus Prince Prey Memorial School? It's disgraceful. But it's a sign of these late times we live in."

"That unfortunate bit of news has indeed reached me. Please do go on," Mr. Luckson implores.

Mr. Scratch growls. "I have said too much already. A pred cannot trust anyone these days." His eyes narrow.

"But you address a fellow pred—one sympathetic to your view, I assure you," soothes Mr. Luckson. "After all, it was my name she removed from the school in favor of their prey hero, and I am none too pleased about it, as you can imagine. You see, I noticed you voiced support for Judge Cavendish's righteous verdict, and I thought perhaps we could help one another. That's why I wanted to meet you."

"That verdict was the best thing to happen in Animal Town in years," replies the fox, his tone softening, "thank the Great Father that preds like Officer Furman and Judge Cavendish still have the courage to uphold the law. And the prey's shameless reaction finally woke a few preds up to what has been happening right under their snouts. I have even had animals attending my temple services again… though I haven't seen *you* there, Mr. Luckson."

"Yes, yes, I am terribly busy. But that is exactly what I wanted to speak with you about. You see, I too am concerned by Dr. Greenbitter's actions and the assault on pred culture in Animal Town. After all, the noble weasel who discovered Animal Town may well be my ancestor. Thus, as a pred, I feel compelled to do my part to support your mission. To wit, I hereby donate twenty-five kilos of shiny rocks to the Great Predator Temple of Animal Town. Perhaps you could use it to build a more modern temple so that our fellow preds might worship the Great Pred Father in an edifice worthy of him."

The weasel was not expecting this. He sits in stunned silence for a moment. Slowly, his eyes begin to sparkle and a smile curls across his lips.

"Why, with twenty-five kilos of shiny rocks… I could even build a school…" he says to himself out loud, looking into the distance beyond his benefactor, lost in the possibilities afforded by capital.

"That's a grand idea my good fox. A private, faith-based school would allow you to save at least some pups, cubs, and eaglets from prey indoctrination. But what about you? We cannot allow you to continue living in an earthen dugout. It's unbecoming an animal of your importance. If you will allow me, I would like to donate a further twenty-five kilos for you to improve your own habitation and to use otherwise as you see fit." Mr. Luckson leans forward, winks, and nods as he speaks.

The fox's eyes bulge with surprise. "Praise the Great Pred Father!" he exclaims. "I prayed for him to send me a sign, and he has answered my prayer! Thank you, Father, and thank you, Mr. Luckson. Your donation will do much to save Animal Town from further spiritual decline, and it has purchased much goodwill from the Pred Father, I assure you."

"Goodwill I am happy to accept, but not publicity," replies Mr. Luckson. "If the prey hear of the source of this donation, I fear they may be emboldened to solicit my shiny rocks for themselves. They are covetous by nature, you know. As such, I must insist on remaining anonymous."

"But of course. You will remain anonymous in this life but will be richly rewarded in the next," Mr. Scratch says, taking Mr. Luckson's paw in his own and shaking it vigorously.

"I have faith that is so. Now, I bid you go and preach the word of our Great Pred Father and build a temple worthy of him."

Thus the interview ends. Mr. Scratch departs Luckson Manor in high spirits and laden with fifty kilos of shiny rocks. The very next day, work begins on the new and improved Great Predator Temple and School of Animal Town.

CHAPTER 9

Winter days pass. The moon waxes and wanes. The season is nearly over, though Animal Town has only grown colder. It has been three weeks since Jack was killed, and Floppy continues to grieve his dead father. The shock and disbelief that dominated his mind immediately after the event have transformed into a sickly throbbing in the pit of his stomach, as though he is constantly on the verge of vomiting. Sleep is his only relief. In waking hours, the dull ache has been punctuated by open sobbing during rare minutes when Floppy is alone with his thoughts.

Anger, too, salts Floppy's grief and ensures its preservation. He is angry at the Lucksons for having more wealth and freedom than his family, angry at Officer Furman for killing his father, and angry at Judge Cavendish for ruling unjustly. Further, fed by Dr. Greenbitter's ongoing lectures, his specific grievances with these predators have metastasized into a more systemic bitterness. Floppy has learned to resent predators in general, and he has begun to see specism everywhere. As a result, his friendship with Charlie has strained. They have seldom spoken and have not played pawball together since the incident.

Floppy's impressionable young mind has been fixated on specism not only by his schoolmaster but also by his employer: The Animal Times. Shortly after the tragic event, Avery asked Dr. Greenbitter to recommend a clever and enterprising student to work for him part-time. She assured him Floppy is the best animal for the job, and he has been working for Avery since.

The savvy goose is glad to have Floppy, for, after years in decline, his newspaper business is now booming. Seizing an opportunity to return to profitability in the wake of the incident, Avery has shifted The Animal Times' focus from reporting dry statistics and unbiased analysis in favor of emotionally charged anecdotes of prey oppression. Editorials written by Dr. Greenbitter and other self-styled "animal justice warriors" fill out the pages on slower news days. Avery has discovered that triggering an emotional response, especially a negative one, is key to driving reader interest. Animals would rather feel bad than feel nothing. Thus, his prey readers are outraged at the injustices The Times reports, while his pred readers are outraged by The Times' anti-pred bias.

As for Floppy, after the loss of his father's income caused his family to slip still deeper into poverty, he is eager to support his mother and siblings any way that he can. For Avery and The Animal Times, he performs a variety of functions, from formatting and researching articles to tracking down leads and investigating potential stories. He is busily formatting the next day's paper when Avery enters the newsroom, in the middle of which sits

Floppy's tidy desk.

"How's this headline: *Coffee Shop Manager Fired for Species Profiling*," Floppy asks as Avery waddles up, his wings folded across his chest.

"Not bad," says the goose, "but it needs a better hook... Hmm, how about, *Coffee Shop Specism: Subconscious Prejudice to Blame?*"

"You got it boss. I can fit that on the front-page layout. No problem," says Floppy, eagerly.

"Great. Run it then," commands the editor. "And when that's done I have a new assignment for you."

Floppy looks up from the layout in anticipation.

"We're doing a piece on the rise of pred supremacy since the... er, well, you know. Anyway, I want you to do the preliminary investigation. Go to the countryside and find some pred supremacists who are willing to discuss their beliefs on record. Try to find the most threatening species you can, like mountain lions, wolves, or coyotes. Gather quotes and any other useful information you can. I'll write the article, but, if you do a good job, I'll include you on the byline."

"Gee thanks, Mr. Avery! I won't let you down!" This is Floppy's first chance to earn a writing credit. He is apprehensive about interviewing pred supremacists, but he is determined to win his boss's approval, nevertheless. As hours of light yet remain in the late winter day, he hastily updates the front-page layout with the new headline and then sets out for the countryside on his bicycle.

Floppy's destination is the Farmers' Co-op and Seed Store a few kilometers outside of town. It is located at the intersection of the main westbound highway and the rural ring road that pred farmers use to travel back and forth from the fields. He has seldom visited the countryside—the last time was when he was a young kit—but Avery assured him that the Co-op is a popular pred hangout.

The Farmers' Co-op and Seed Store is a ramshackle wooden building, dating from the turn of the last century. The latest layer of white paint, applied more than 20 years ago, chips haphazardly from its exterior. A rusted gas pump of antique provenance stands before its low porch, upon which two old farmers sit drinking coffee. One is an eagle wearing a sweat-stained mesh ball cap with a seed company logo on the front. His companion is a grizzled weasel, missing more than a few teeth. Into one of the gaps in his mouth fits a cigarette, which sags with surprise when its smoker sees a young Jackrabbit ride up on a bicycle.

"Good evening, gentle-animals," Floppy says pleasantly as he mounts the steps to the porch, squelching his inner disdain. "My name is Floppy, and I am with The Animal Times. Could I please ask you a few questions?"

"Concernin' what?" asks the weasel, peering through narrow eyes and puffing his cigarette.

"We are doing a story on the reaction to the recent killing within the predator community. I'd love to hear your thoughts."

The two preds eye one another for a moment before the weasel speaks up.

"Well, I don't wanna see my name in that dern paper of yers, but I don't mind telling ya it hasn't made a lick of difference out here. I know the city prey are gettin' their fur in knots about it, but we country animals can't afford to worry about one less jackrabbit in Animal Town. We've got families to feed and chores enough of our own. Heck, it'll be plantin' time again soon and—"

"Why don't you speak for yer ownself, Clem?" interrupts the eagle. "*You* may not be able to work and think about politics in one go, but I sure as shoot can."

Floppy takes out his pad and pen. This seems to boost the eagle's confidence; he continues with more authority.

"Most animals carry on with their business, that's true, Clem, but what about all those preds who started going to ol' Scratch's Temple? Why, we ain't seen that since my father was a chick, I reckon. Anyway, there's more'n a few preds who are none too pleased about that new schoolmaster they got in town or about what you've been printing in yer paper—pred justice and such nonsense."

"Please continue, sir," prods Floppy.

"Well, I don't want my name in yer paper either, but Fleischbauer's inside, and I bet he'll talk that big ear of yers right off if you let him."

"Thanks for the tip. He's inside you say? How will I know him?"

"Just go on in, and ya can't miss 'im. He's the biggest gol-dern grey wolf you ever saw, I reckon." With this, the eagle turns back to his weasel companion, and the two begin discussing the unusually cold weather.

Taking the hint, Floppy thanks the two preds for their time and opens the outer screen and inner wooden doors to the Co-op. He steps inside, inadvertently letting the screen door slam shut behind him with a "bang." The sudden noise prompts the animals within to stop and look at the stranger who has entered their midst, a not too frequent occurrence.

Floppy shudders involuntarily, causing his fur to bristle. He looks about the store. To the left are the seed counter and several aisles stocked with various farm supplies that look bizarre to Floppy's urban eyes. A middle-aged coyote wearing a smock stands behind the counter. In one of the aisles, father and son weasels paw a new scoop shovel. To the right is the café, containing three rustic wooden booths along the back wall and three tables by the window. Two lions, a bear, and an enormous grey wolf fill one of the booths. A chubby vixen waits on them. With Floppy's entry, all conversation stops, and keen predator eyes fix on him for perhaps two seconds. Then the animals continue where they had left off, as if a young jackrabbit were not among them.

Floppy sighs with relief. He is unused to being the only prey among so many preds. "I am a reporter," he tells himself. "This is the job." Attempting to hide his nerves and ignoring the sickly feeling in his stomach, Floppy strides boldly towards the threateningly occupied booth. The animals do not acknowledge him, though he stands almost within their grasp.

"Excuse me," he says, looking at the wolf. "I am sorry to bother you gentle-animals. My name is Floppy, and I am a reporter with The Animal Times. I'm working on a story, and a nice eagle outside said I should speak with a mister, ah, Mr. Fleischbauer."

"Yeah, I'm Fleischbauer. What of it?" says the wolf, looking once more at Floppy. He is much larger than an average wolf, bigger even than the black bear sitting opposite. His forepaws, the left of which is missing two digits from a farming accident, are the size of melons when clenched. He wears a checkered flannel shirt and faded blue jeans.

Floppy's fur bristles again when he meets Fleischbauer's gaze. "Well s-s-sir," he stammers. "The Times is doing a story on the pred reaction to the recent killing and Judge Cavendish's verdict. I would be grateful for a few minutes to interview you about it."

"Justice served. That's my reaction," the wolf says flatly. "And you can tell that prey-loving editor of yours Fleischbauer said so."

Anger and sadness churn undigested in Floppy's belly. He tries to ignore them and takes a deep breath before continuing his questioning.

"I'll quote you on that, sir. Thank you. What about animals attending the Great Predator Temple? Have you visited yourself?"

"Sure have. I was there the first weekend after the verdict, and I have been going twice a week since. Ol' Scratch is the first one with the guts to say in public what a lot of us have been thinking. I respect that, and I'm not the only one either. There must have been fifty preds there last weekend—had to have the service outdoors. Now that the new temple's going up, there'll soon be more. I intend to send my youngest pup to the school as well, soon as he's old enough. My eldest is already at ATU, you know."

Jotting notes hastily, Floppy inquires further. "And what exactly does Mr. Scratch say at the temple that you and other preds find appealing?"

"The truth, simple as that: he says we have forgotten the word of the Pred Father who teaches us to stick to our own, worship and serve only him, and have faith in our salvation in the next life. He says mixing pred and prey species has caused Animal Town to decline, and that pred culture is under attack. He says preds ought to be in charge of Animal Town, and that we've got to make sure the next mayor is on our side. He says prey are lazy and criminal by nature, and it's no surprise they have resorted to lawlessness and thievery. He says Animal Town would descend into anarchy if not for a few good preds like Officer Furman and Judge Cavendish, who stand up for pred rights. And… he says that filthy rabbit got what he deserved."

Fleischbauer gives Floppy a malicious sneer. His specist insults cause the stew of anger in Floppy's stomach to boil into a rage that catches in his throat. He copies the wolf's vitriol verbatim, trying to distract himself from his emotions by focusing on his work. He fears he might burst into tears and embarrass himself.

The lions and bear seated with Fleischbauer smile and chuckle impudently at his remarks. The waitress, looking inquisitively at Floppy, frowns as she wipes the table of the adjacent booth. Seeing that the young hare is on the verge of tears, the brawny wolf adds, nonchalantly, "No offense to you personally, of course."

"Of course. So you hate prey because Mr. Scratch tells you to?" Floppy manages to ask, through clenched teeth.

"Well, since you asked: I hate prey because they hate me. The city prey all look down on us rural preds, think they're better than us. Mayor Middleton, with his highfalutin talk, thinks we're all stupid. And that ewe Camilla comes out here every new moon, dressed in her fancy clothes and robs us of every last shiny rock. I want to see Animal Town the way it was back in my grandpa's day, back when the prey showed us some respect and working animals could afford to live decently."

The kindly waitress has listened unobtrusively from beside the booth. Her arms are folded across her apron, and she wears concern on her face.

"Just you take it easy there, Fleischbauer," the vixen interjects. "You're speakin' to a jackrabbit after all, and I don't 'preciate you being rude to my customers, prey or not." Turning to Floppy, she continues, "I'm sorry 'bout that youngin. I'll get you a soda, on the house." While Floppy continues scribbling notes, she scurries behind the counter and quickly returns with a dripping soda bottle in paw. "Here you go, son," she says as she smoothes the fur on the back of his neck with her paw. "You didn't happen to know the jackrabbit that was killed, did ya?"

Floppy takes a big gulp of the cool soda. The carbonation tickles his whiskers, and the caffeine steadies his nerves. "He was my fa…"

"Bang," the screen door slams, and again heads involuntarily turn, Floppy's included. A young coyote strides through the doorway, barely noticing the animals within. It is Charlie, come to fetch a bag of seed for his father.

Recognizing his erstwhile friend and grateful for the opportunity to terminate the interview, Floppy hastily thanks Fleischbauer for his time and makes a line for

Charlie. The juvenile coyote stands at the seed counter. "...order was one bag short. It's listed under Clawson, my father..." he is saying to the clerk when Floppy, unnoticed, taps him on the shoulder.

Charlie turns and smiles curiously at the surprise that confronts him. "Floppy? What are you doing here?" he gets out before Floppy cuts in.

"Hiya, stranger. Surprised to see me? I'm here working on a story."

"Oh, right—The Animal Times. What kind of story brings you to the countryside? From what I've read all The Times seems to care about lately is if the next mayor will be a prey, or if enough prey are accepted to ATU, or if a pred dresses up as a prey for a costume party."

"Actually, it's about pred supremacy, and I guess I came to the right place. I just got an earful of it from that big wolf over there, but don't look now." Floppy speaks in a hushed voice.

"Pred supremacy!" Charlie exclaims, loud enough for the café to hear and causing the animals therein to stare.

"Shh! You're gonna get me in a jam," whispers Floppy. "Yes, pred supremacy. Avery, my boss, thinks it's on the rise since that bastard bear murdered my father."

"I should have known," Charlie says absently. The clerk returns from the back of the store and hauls a bag of seed onto the counter. "Thanks, Bill. We're all square now." Turning to Floppy, he says: "Well, since you're here, you might as well help me carry this seed out to my truck. Grab that end."

The boys carry the seed bag outside and heave it into the back of Charlie's rusted work pickup.

"Where are you going to dig up more pred dirt now?" Charlie asks as he closes the tailgate.

"Well, the Co-op was my only lead, other than the Temple. But it's too late to get there before dark, so I guess I'll just go home."

"Well, if you don't mind being seen with a pred, I can give you a ride. I just need to drop the seed off at my den first. You can finally see where I live."

Floppy assents. They load his bicycle into the truck bed and are soon cruising through the countryside in serene late winter dusk. Charlie lives some twenty kilometers from the Co-op. The remoteness of his farm has prevented Floppy from visiting sooner but today affords him the opportunity to observe how preds in the countryside live. Floppy stares out the window inquisitively as the two animals bounce down the potholed dirt road in awkward silence for several minutes. In the fading light, they pass a farm every few kilometers. Floppy is surprised to see the farmhouses in ramshackle condition. Not unlike his family's shanty in town, all are in various states of disrepair.

Some have boarded windows, others are missing shingles or have crumbling chimneys, and most have not seen fresh paint in decades. Old wooden barns tilt precariously, rusted tractors dissolve in the corners of fields, and beat-up pickup trucks park in gravel driveways. These preds are a far cry from the opulence of Luckson Manor.

It is not what Floppy expected to see. Over the last few weeks, he has formed the impression that all preds are better off than his own family. After all, Dr. Greenbitter taught him that predators have more freedom than prey, and Mr. Luckson's example taught him to equate wealth with freedom. But these country preds are certainly not wealthy. Indeed, Floppy thinks to himself, if their houses were clustered together, they would form a shantytown much like that in which his family dwells.

"That's my den up ahead," Charlie interrupts Floppy's musing. Moments later, he turns down a driveway and parks in front of his family's pale blue farmhouse. Floppy notices that it has shifted slightly on its foundation, leaving a crack of air between the front door and its frame. "Help me carry the seed to the barn, will ya?" the coyote asks the jackrabbit.

Walking to the barn, Floppy says, "You know, Charlie, your den looks just like mine. And all those other houses we passed could have been my neighbors. I figured you were all living in luxury out here."

Charlie frowns. "Yeah, it's not exactly how Dr. Greenbitter and The Times tell it, is it? I keep wonderin' how I can get some of that pred privilege they're always on about. You ask that boss of yours for me the next time you see him."

"I just might do that. Maybe we could do a story on rural poverty or something. I think most of the prey in Animal Town would be surprised, too," Floppy says thoughtfully.

"I know one who won't be surprised: Ms. Camilla. She comes out here every new moon to collect rent. Why Mr. Luckson sends a prey for the job is beyond me. Anyway, she sees how rural preds live, but it doesn't stop her collectin' every gram of shiny rock. You know, a couple months ago my parents were a little behind, so they had me go into town to drop off some premium hay at Camilla's house to try to buy us some time. I can tell you that sheep lives almost as high as Mr. Luckson. She's got a nice, big house on the east side of town, where the pheasants and sheep live. They all seem to be much better off than the preds out here, if you ask me. Anyway, I gave her the hay, but she still charged us double the shiny rocks the next month!"

At this moment, the idea growing in Floppy's mind begins to bud. Soon after this exchange the two young animals are back in Charlie's pickup, heading for the prey shantytown. Their conversation is lighter now. They talk of girls, the future, and pawball. Both agree it has been too long since they played together, and they resolve to do so again soon.

CHAPTER 10

After school the next day, Floppy rushes to The Animal Times' office. Once there, he hurriedly finishes the layout and slips out again without even speaking to Avery. He is supposed to continue researching the pred supremacy article; he is supposed to find specists to interview at the Great Predator Temple. But the idea budding in his mind urges him elsewhere. Exiting the building, he mounts his bicycle and pedals east.

As Mr. Hoofman alluded in his farewell lecture, Animal Town is a land of immigrants. All the predator species' ancestors emigrated from the West, while most of the prey species' ancestors emigrated or were brought as slaves from the South. However, on the east side of Animal Town, where Floppy is headed, are clustered the prey species whose ancestors emigrated from the East. Though their forebears were not formally enslaved like many of the southern prey, they, too, were once exploited by the preds, and they were even denied citizenship and the right to own property. These eastern prey—ring-necked pheasants and bighorn sheep—are the least numerous species in Animal Town. While approximately sixty percent of citizens are predators and thirty-five percent are southern prey, only about five percent are eastern prey.

Floppy is surprised when he arrives at their neighborhood and sees the truth of what Charlie has told him. If their living conditions are any indication, the eastern prey are doing very well indeed. Their homes are large and well maintained, with landscaped lawns and shiny new cars. Camilla's house, in particular, is impressive. To Floppy's eyes, it appears a small-scale Luckson Manor. These prey are a far cry from the rural poverty Floppy witnessed the day before, as well as the shantytown where he lives among the southern prey.

The clever young jackrabbit pedals up and down the streets for about an hour, all the while lost in thought. *How have these prey managed to do so well?* he ponders, *and why haven't I heard about it before? They cannot benefit from pred privilege, and yet they are wealthy and free all the same...* Such thoughts occupy his mind as he pedals back to The Animal Times office.

At his desk once more, Floppy puts the investigative skills Avery has taught him to use. On his computer, he looks up Animal Town education attainment and household income statistics and sorts them by species. Pouring over the statistics, he begins to see that there is a strong, positive relationship between education and wealth. Pheasants and sheep tend to be better educated than other species, including preds, and they also tend to be wealthier. Indeed, when Floppy sorts occupation statistics by species, he finds, relative to their small population, eastern prey produce a great many of the town's doctors, engineers, and ATU professors. *Might this be the link between knowledge and freedom that Mr. Hoofman was talking about?* he wonders to himself. The earnest young jackrabbit is so focused on his work that he does not notice when Avery silently waddles up behind him and watches over his shoulder. After a few moments, the goose asks, "What are you working on there, Floppy? You're supposed to be down at the Temple interviewing pred supremacists."

Floppy starts in his chair. He gathers himself and, turning to face his boss, says, "Did you know that pheasants and sheep are better educated and earn more rocks than any other species in Animal Town, even preds?"

"What? Where did you hear that?" says the goose, with concern.

"I didn't hear it anywhere. I found it out for myself. Look, I've got the numbers right here. See for yourself."

Avery leans in to inspect the computer screen. What Floppy says is true. The data are clear, and they do not lie.

"Hmm…," says the goose, shrugging his wings and darting his eyes about the room. "I guess you're right. That *is* a surprise."

"Well, what are we going to do about it? This is important. Animals need to know," Floppy says eagerly, trying to meet Avery's eyes.

"Do about it? What do you mean *do about it*? What is there to do?"

"This is a newspaper, isn't it? Well, this is news. We need to get it into print. You taught me that journalists have a duty to report the unbiased truth. So, that's what we should do."

"Now hold on just a minute there, kito. I'm the editor of this paper, and I decide what counts as news. Right now, I say pred supremacy is news, and that's what I told you to report on. What are you doing digging up statistics anyway? If you want to earn that writing credit, you better get back on the pred supremacy story and forget about all these *numbers*."

Floppy is becoming agitated. The sickly feeling in his stomach is rising again. "B-but, sir," he stammers, "these *numbers* contradict what we've been reporting for the last three weeks. This is hard evidence that pred supremacy and specism can't be the only thing holding prey back. Animals have a right to know the truth!"

"They have a right to know what I tell them!" Avery is angry now and practically shouting. "I'm warning you Floppy: don't shock the flock. Paper sales have never been better, and I'm not going to let a few boring statistics ruin that for me. I tried that once, and I almost went out of business. And don't you lecture me about journalistic integrity. We *do* print the truth at the Times, the truth of individual animals' lived experiences. Your statistics can never convey the depth of emotion their stories can. Now drop this and get back to work on the pred supremacy story!"

Floppy sits in stunned silence, his mouth agape and eyes open wide, welling with tears. Seconds slip slowly as the two animals stare at each other, unblinking. Then, suddenly, Floppy's idea bursts into bloom.

"I quit," he says. So spontaneously does he speak that he surprises even himself. But he knows he has done the right thing, for the knot in his stomach immediately loosens, unwinding the bitterness and anger that has poisoned him against preds. Deep in his subconscious, he begins to forgive Officer Furman for killing his father. For the first time, he sees the bear not simply as a specist predator, bent on oppressing prey, but instead as an individual animal who made a mistake in a fraught situation. He instantly feels lighter, unburdened, happy even. He lets go of his grievances and makes peace with the circumstances of his life that he cannot change. He acknowledges that he cannot alter the past or choose his fate, but he accepts responsibility for his future nonetheless. For the first time in his life, he is free. A wide grin spreads across his face. Before Avery has time to reply, Floppy is clearing his desk of his belongings and stuffing them into his backpack.

Now the goose watches in stunned silence. He stumbles back from the desk in shock. At length he manages to say, quivering with rage, "You can't quit! Think of your family. You need this job, and you know it!" But Floppy ignores him. He whistles a cheerful tune as he continues packing his things. This pushes Avery beyond the bounds of reason. "You know what? You're fired! Get out of my office and don't come back!" he shouts. "And you better believe Dr. Greenbitter is going to hear about this. Every animal has their price, Floppy!"

But Floppy is already on the way to the door. He pauses for a moment and says, over his shoulder, "Not this animal." Then he continues whistling where he left off, pushes the office door open, and breaths in the fresh air, smiling all the while.

CHAPTER 11

Junior is late for the morning service. He was at the social club the night before, attempting to impress a jill weasel of dubious reputation until well past midnight. Prior to this illicit social engagement, he spent the entire day golfing, and, thus, he struggled to drag himself out of his king-size, four-post bed. By the time Junior finally arrives at the Great Predator Temple of Animal Town, wearing a boxy black suit designed to hide his corpulence, the service has already begun.

The new temple has been under construction for nearly a month, turning the field where Floppy and Charlie once played pawball into an active work zone. Today, for the first time, the weekend service is taking place within. Though, it is not technically indoors, for the temple yet lacks a roof. Nevertheless, more than 100 animals brave the brisk late winter air to fill the rising stone structure, arranged on straight-backed pine pews. Officer Furman is there with his cub Ralph, sitting in the second row. Another of Floppy's classmates, Sylvester, is present with his grey wolf family. The huge wolf Fleischbauer spills into the aisle, his youngest pup at his side but his oldest son absent. At the front of the temple stands the ancient

Mr. Scratch. Sheathed in a black robe, the fox is speaking from the pulpit when Junior slides into the back row, next to a family of coyotes.

Junior is attending at the request of his father. He would rather sleep in and play another round of golf, as is his custom, but his father insisted he attend and report what he sees and hears. Mr. Luckson likes to keep close tabs on his investments, but he prefers to do so from a distance.

As Junior settles into the pew, Mr. Scratch's words drift down the hall to meet his keen weasel ears. "'Be fruitful, and multiply, and replenish the earth, and subdue it:'" intones the fox in his raspy voice, "'and have dominion over the land and sea, and over the air and sky, and over every living thing upon the earth.' Thus spake our Great Pred Father, and thus we preds once did. We spread out to the four corners of the earth, establishing our dominion and bringing the light of civilization to the world. This was our burden, but we bore it nobly, secure in our ancient faith and in the belief that it is our destiny to rule the world. For only when preds are masters will the Great Pred Father Return to Earth to sit in judgment at the end of days. Only then will he welcome we righteous few into his eternal kingdom. This great destiny was once within our grasp; our claws could almost touch it. We were once fruitful and multiplying…"

Predator heads nod in agreement.

"Alas, that era has passed. In these late days, the

strength of pred blood has been diluted by generations of unnatural mixing with prey. We preds, who built and long ruled Animal Town, have ceded leadership without a struggle. We have lost our will to power and succumbed to the slave morality peddled by meek prey species that stand to inherit the earth after our abdication. They say they want a post-species society, but really they want a post-pred society."

The assembled congregation murmurs assent.

"You want proof?" continues Mr. Scratch. "Pay a visit to the maternity ward of Animal Town Hospital if you doubt me. I've been there myself, and I'll tell you what you'll see: you'll see deer and pronghorn fawns, pheasant chicks and goslings, bison calves and lambs, little gopher pups and jackrabbit kits—prey spawn in abundance. But seldom will you hear an eaglet screech; a wolf, coyote, or fox pup cry; or a bear cub groan for its mother's milk. The prey babies must outnumber the preds' three to one. It doesn't take a fancy education to figure out what this means for us, my good preds: it means we're being replaced!"

Again the crowd murmurs, this time with consternation. Heads shake in solemn disapproval.

Junior observes the scene with interest. He sees how Mr. Scratch holds the preds spellbound—how the older animals' eyes glisten with a far-off look when the preacher speaks of better times, long past. Throughout the remainder of the service, he wonders how he might turn their enthusiasm to his advantage.

Meanwhile, Mr. Scratch leads the congregation through a series of rituals that require the animals to variously sit, stand, or kneel; to sing songs, and repeat incantations. After perhaps forty minutes, the theatrics of the service are at an end, and Mr. Scratch makes his closing announcements.

"My pred brothers and sisters," he rasps. "I remind you that that meddlesome gopher, the so-called *Doctor* Greenbitter, is giving a lecture this evening at Animal Town University. I will be there to protest her anti-pred propaganda, and I hope to see you all there as well. We must send a strong message that preds will not be bowled over without a fight. Furthermore, I expect to see all of you at the town meeting tomorrow night and at the election the following day. We must stick together to nominate and elect a mayor who will protect pred rights. Political power is the only path back to the Promised Land!"

Junior's ears perk at the mention of "election," "mayor," and "political power." Suddenly he sees a means by which to satisfy his own lust for fame and adulation and to make his father proud at the same time. He lingers after the service ends and the other animals have finally departed.

Then he approaches the old fox saying, "Have I got a deal for you, ol' Scratch, probably the best deal in history..."

Camilla is early for the lecture. Mr. Luckson asked her to attend, but she would have come even if he had not. She has been reading Dr. Greenbitter's editorials in The Times over the past month, and she is eager to make the young gopher's acquaintance. Like her boss, the ambitious sheep sees an opportunity to exploit prey grievances to serve her own ends.

Mr. Luckson's bison chauffer drops Camilla on the street in front of Animal Town University lecture hall. She knows the campus well from her days as a student and from visiting her parents who professed there. A wave of fond memories washes over her as she trots up the sidewalk toward the hall.

A scene without parallel in her memory, however, confronts her when she nears the entrance. Several dozen predators are clustered along each side of the walk, behind security cordons running along its length. Many are carrying signs bearing slogans which they shout as she walks past.

"You will not replace us!" a wolf howls.

"Go back to where you came from!" screeches an eagle.

Mr. Scratch is there leading the pack. He sneers viciously at Camilla with squinting yellow eyes and bared fangs. Camilla shivers. Then, just before the campus security bison bundles her into the hall, she spots a portly weasel in a sack suit standing beside the graying red fox. *Isn't that Junior?* she asks herself. *What's he doing here?*

She has no time to find out, though, for, once inside, she is immediately confronted with the object of her mission. Dr. Greenbitter sits behind a table in the foyer, upon which are piled posters, coffee mugs, and sweatshirts, all emblazoned with the slogan, *Prey Lives Matter*. Dr. Greenbitter and the ATU faculty sitting at either side of her appear to be doing a brisk trade in the merchandise, which the young schoolmaster will autograph for an additional five grams of shiny rocks. Camilla approaches the table, smiling, and dressed in her best business suit.

"Good evening, Dr. Greenbitter," she bleats. "I have been so looking forward to your lecture. Please allow me to introduce myself: my name is Camilla and…"

"Oh, I know who you are," the gopher interrupts. "It's an honor to finally meet you. I had class with both your parents. They were wonderful professors. Your family's success is an inspiration to the prey of Animal Town." She grasps Camilla's forehoof and shakes it enthusiastically with both paws.

"You're too kind, but thank you. Truth be told, I'm a fan of *yours*: I have been following your articles in The Times from the beginning. You have given a voice to the marginalized species of Animal Town—I love your glasses, by the way."

"Why, thank you; they're vintage," says the gopher.

"Well they're lovely," says the sheep. "I'm so glad to meet you, for I am eager to do my part in the fight for animal justice. Do you have some time to discuss how we might combine forces? As Mr. Luckson's right paw animal, I can bring considerable influence to bear."

"That sounds wonderful, Camilla. The prey cause would benefit hugely from the support of an animal of your stature. But my lecture is about to begin. May we continue the conversation after?"

"Yes, of course, Dr. Greenbitter. I'll wait for you."

"Excellent. Why don't we meet in the ready room backstage? We can chat privately there. I believe this is the beginning of a powerful alliance!" says the gopher, finally releasing the sheep's hoof.

Exiting the foyer, Camilla enters the hall and finds her seat among the more than 100 animals within. Most are prey, but there are several pred students and professors mixed in, a large grey wolf conspicuous among them. Avery sits in the front row, holding an audio recorder. Young Cassie, noticeable with her dark wool, is there with her family, as are several other prey classmates and their families. But Floppy and his mother are absent. Lil is working late at the shiny rock mine, and Floppy is at his new job. He now works as a hired paw at Charlie's family farm.

After a few minutes, the lights dim, and a tall, lean buck takes the podium, prompting the chattering crowd to fall silent.

"May I have your attention, please?" says the bespectacled deer, wearing a corduroy blazer over his wiry frame. "As the chair of the prey studies department at ATU, it is my distinct honor to introduce an animal most worthy of our esteem, an animal who has alerted us to systemic specism and pred supremacy in Animal Town— and a distinguished alumna or our own department, I might add. She is here tonight to deliver an important and timely lecture entitled, 'The Case for Retribution.' Please join me in welcoming ATU's own, Dr. Greenbitter!"

Applause rains down as Dr. Greenbitter strides across the stage and warmly embraces her former professor. Amidst the clapping hooves, the ten-point buck trots off stage, and the gopher steps up to the podium. Her beaming smile slowly melts into a stern expression as she adjusts the microphone lower, clears her throat, and begins to speak in a high, squeaky voice.

"It is an honor to be invited to speak at my alma mater and a pleasure to address an audience composed of so many friendly prey faces. Thank you for being here and for supporting the fight for animal justice. I see that there are also a few pred faces among us. Thank you for being allies of our cause and for setting the example for your species. I request that you listen and learn how to begin the work of dismantling pred supremacy and atoning for your ancestral guilt."

Dr. Greenbitter adjusts her hollow eyeglass frames and continues.

"Would that a few good preds were enough to wash away the bloody legacy of violence and oppression that stains each newborn pred with Animal Town's original sin. Would that pred contrition suffice to rectify the injustices upon which our town was founded and which continue to this day. Would that repentance was enough to atone for pred guilt."

The gopher shakes her head mournfully.

"Alas, it is insufficient merely to rectify past wrongs, to make equal what was once unequal, to forgive and forget. No, that will not do. An apology and an end to oppression are not enough. We prey will not embrace preds as brothers and sisters and go merrily on our way. No, we will not. Prey demand more, for the only remedy to past discrimination is present discrimination; and the only remedy to present discrimination is future discrimination. As such, animal justice requires not only the cessation of injustice but its reversal. Animal justice requires *retribution!*"

The crowd applauds enthusiastically. Many ungulates stamp their hooves and low in agreement. Looking gratified, Dr. Greenbitter waits for the echo of the last clap before continuing, speaking louder now.

"No my prey friends, the victims of eight generations of slavery, political exclusion, and quiet plunder have not been made whole by two generations of relative freedom and so-called equality. Victimhood is our species' inheritance, and each newborn or hatched prey is embittered anew by past oppression. Though I was not alive to experience it myself, I yet feel the pain suffered by my ancestors at the paws of their pred oppressors. Animal justice demands this pain be repaid, with interest. The retribution must fit the crime!"

Cheers rise once more. Dr. Greenbitter is now shouting into the microphone.

"I say that the struggle for animal justice did not begin with the murder of one jackrabbit, nor will it end when Officer Furman and Judge Cavendish are finally made to pay for their crimes. No my prey friends, the struggle began when the first enslaved prey set hoof in Animal Town, and it will not end until prey have ruled Animal Town unchallenged for eight generations!"

Dr. Greenbitter pounds her clenched paw on the podium to punctuate the last line. The crowd breaks into a raucous din of clapping and clomping, rattling the glass light fixtures swinging overhead. Camilla, too, is caught up in the emotions of the herd. She whistles through her cloven forehoof and stomps in approval.

After some seconds basking in the warm glow of adulation, the young gopher raises her paws, indicating her desire for quiet. The herd obeys.

"In closing, my prey friends and pred allies, I remind you that we are in the midst of a fateful moment in Animal Town's history. At the town meeting tomorrow night, we shall nominate candidates for mayor, and on the following day one of the candidates shall be elected. It is our grave duty to ensure that a prey animal committed to our cause is nominated and elected mayor. Only with political power can we begin the program of retribution! Only with political power can we begin to extract payment on the accumulated debt of eight generations of pred supremacy! I say retribution *now*, retribution *tomorrow*, and retribution *forever!*"

Cheers rise yet again. Dr. Greenbitter shouts through the din into the mic.

"Vote prey or betray your species, my friends! And you preds: vote prey to make a small down payment on your species' debt! Retribution is within our grasp!"

The crowd stands and delivers a stirring ovation. Camilla rises, too, clapping with gusto. Then she slides down the row to the side aisle and walks towards the stage. Applause continues as she slips through a side door and finds her way to the ready room back stage.

Inside she finds various prey food and drinks strewn across a sumptuous buffet. She helps herself to the spread and sits down to wait for Dr. Greenbitter.

In the lecture hall, the deluge of applause eventually subsides, and Camilla can just hear the department chair begin fielding questions from the audience on Dr. Greenbitter's behalf.

The first animal called on has a youthful voice. "Thanks

for the awesome lecture, Dr. Greenbitter." *He must be a student*, Camilla guesses. "My question is: don't we already have political power? I mean, Mayor Middleton is a prey, right?"

"How about that, Doctor?" says the refined buck. "What's your take on Mayor Middleton?"

"I expected this question," she responds, coolly. "Mayor Middleton is a good animal. I think we can all agree on that, but the fact is he was not the agent of change that many of us hoped he would be. He was not willing to implement the retribution that animal justice requires. Let's not forget that he was adopted and raised by wolves and must have internalized pred culture as a result. That is why it's imperative his successor be a true animal justice warrior and not a wolf in pronghorn hide."

Backstage, Camilla smiles with self-satisfaction, munching on fresh, premium hay. She knows just how to turn Dr. Greenbitter's zealotry to her advantage. A few minutes later when the urbane young gopher enters the ready room, Camilla greets her saying, "Dr. Greenbitter, I have a proposition for you…"

Camilla and Dr. Greenbitter are in such close conversation that they do not even notice the commotion outside the lecture hall. As attendees file outside, they are confronted by a mob of angry preds cursing and shouting slogans at them, including their favorite: "You will not replace us!"

The prey respond with their own chants: "Prey lives matter! Prey lives matter!" A pushing match ensues across the flimsy cordon separating the species. In the front rank the aged Mr. Scratch rallies the preds, though Junior is no longer at his side. He has slipped to the rear of the pack, prioritizing his own safety. Nevertheless, he instigates his fellow preds at full voice, promising, "I'll pay the legal fees of any pred who knocks the manure out of a prey!" Avery, likewise, observes and records from a safe distance.

The scuffle continues for several minutes and is on the verge of violence when a golf cart bearing the campus security officer arrives. The brown bison rapidly imposes his bulk between the hostile groups, preventing the situation coming to blows. Moments later a police cruiser with sirens blaring jumps the curb onto the lawn in front of the hall. Out steps Officer Furman with a megaphone.

"You are ordered to disperse!" he commands. "If you do not disperse in thirty seconds, you will be tear gassed!"

Furman's threat has the desired effect. The crowd soon begins breaking up in their various directions, west, east, and south, as the case may be. Many animals continue shouting and chanting as they back away from the fight.

More than an hour later, Camilla and Dr. Greenbitter

emerge, unaware.

CHAPTER 12

VOTE PREY OR BETRAY! exclaims The Animal Times' front-page headline the following morning. Below the headline, the text of Dr. Greenbitter's lecture is printed in full. An article on *The Resurgence of Pred Supremacy*, written by Avery, appears on the second page. Extrapolating from Floppy's abandoned research, Avery chronicles the "rampant" specism among rural preds and the "worrying" growth of the Great Predator Temple congregation. Other articles describe the predators' aggressive provocations after the lecture and speculate on which prey might be nominated for mayor. To keep up with demand since the fateful incident, Avery has more than doubled the number of papers printed each day; this edition sells out nevertheless.

Fueled in part by The Animal Times, the atmosphere is combustible as animals gather at Animal Town Hall and Courthouse for their monthly meeting, at which they will nominate mayoral candidates. Save for Mr. Luckson and Judge Cavendish, who are in seclusion together at Luckson Manor, all the adult citizens are present. The hall is once again packed with tense animals well before the appointed time, and their self-segregation is even more thorough. The right of the hall is entirely preds. The left is almost entirely prey; as at the lecture the night before, only a few preds affiliated with ATU sit among them. The two sides scarcely look at one another as they wait impatiently for the meeting to begin.

Mr. Hoofman, whom outgoing Mayor Middleton appointed to preside at the meeting, sits next to the center aisle in the left front row, rubbing his temples with his forehooves. The bison has aged markedly in the past month. He has lost weight, and, betokening his enfeeblement, his once intimidating beard is now entirely gray. He looks at his watch and sighs deeply, his broad shoulders slumping. The time has come to discharge his duty. Slowly and deliberately he stands, saunters up to the stage, and approaches the historic oaken podium. The murmuring animals fall silent, closely regarding the respected former schoolmaster.

"This meeting is not about me," says the old bull, with a note of exasperation in his shaky voice, "so, for the time being, I will forego a longwinded speech and proceed directly to the business at hand. Though, as the duly appointed officiant of these proceedings, I reserve the right to intervene at any time to ensure their orderly conduct.

"The task before us is to nominate two candidates for mayor, one of whom will be elected tomorrow, on the first day of spring, as our tradition demands. The polls open at sunrise, and the votes will be counted by Judge Cavendish at high noon. Thank you for coming tonight, and I urge you to fulfill your civic duty by voting tomorrow.

"The nomination procedure is as follows: I will call for a nomination from among the animals present. If the nomination is seconded and accepted by the nominee, the candidate is thereby officially nominated. I will then repeat the procedure as many times as a nomination is made, seconded, and accepted. If more than two candidates are nominated, we will vote by show of forelimbs to determine the top two. Is that understood?"

Heads nod perfunctorily.

"Very well. Do I hear a nomination?"

From the numerous garbled pred and prey voices that reach Mr. Hoofman's drooping ears, he discerns nominations for Dr. Greenbitter and Mr. Scratch.

"One at a time, one at a time," he scolds. "I believe I hear a nomination for Dr. Greenbitter. Do I hear a second?"

"Second!" responds the prey chorus.

"Boo!" shout the preds.

Dr. Greenbitter does not react.

"Order if you please. No more outbursts, no more outbursts," says Mr. Hoofman, weakly. "Dr. Greenbitter, you have been nominated and seconded. Do you accept the nomination?"

Silence in the hall.

"I respectfully decline," says the young gopher.

Gasps, then silence. Preds and prey look about confusedly.

"Very well. Mr. Scratch has also been nominated. Do I hear a second?"

"Second!" from the pred chorus.

"And do *you* accept the nomination, Mr. Scratch?"

"Decline," says the old fox.

Gasps again. The air within the hall grows thin.

The bison emits a guttural snort and furrows his brows. "So be it. Do I hear any *other* nominations?"

Pregnant silence reigns and heads turn in unison, in opposite directions. The prey look to the left front row where sits Dr. Greenbitter, flanked by Avery and Camilla and backed by ATU faculty and school board members. The preds look to the right front row where sits Mr. Scratch, flanked by Officer Furman and Junior and backed by Fleischbauer and the rural preds. Both the herd and pack await direction from their leaders. Perhaps assuming the honor is his by right of seniority, Mr. Scratch is first to speak.

"I nominate Mr. Luckson Jr.," he says, curtly.

"Second," says Officer Furman, almost before Mr. Scratch ceases speaking.

"Fine," says Mr. Hoofman. "And do you accept, Mr. Luckson Jr.?"

Standing and facing the pred crowd, Junior replies, "I accept, and I'm going to be the best mayor in Animal Town history, big time. A lot of animals have told me I should be mayor, and, believe me, I'm the only animal who can put the prey back in their place and the preds back in charge!"

The preds clap and cheer. Mr. Hoofman frowns again. "That's quite enough, Mr. Luckson, quite enough. Each candidate will have an opportunity to make a speech once the nomination process is complete." The cheers subside and the bison continues his weighty task.

"Mr. Luckson Jr. has been nominated. Do I hear another?"

"I hereby nominate the next mayor of Animal Town, Ms. Camilla the sheep," squeaks Dr. Greenbitter.

"And I second the nomination," says Avery.

Now it is the prey's turn to cheer. Mr. Hoofman waits impatiently. "So be it," he says at last. "Do you accept the nomination, Ms. Camilla?"

"I humbly accept the honor my gracious peers have seen fit to bestow upon me," she replies.

"Very well," says the bull. "We have the required two nominees. Do I hear any additional nominations?"

Calm is briefly restored as the animals wait for the formalities to be completed. There will be no more nominations. The combatants are chosen.

"That settles it then," says Mr. Hoofman, dejectedly, after several seconds of silence. "We have our candidates for the office of Mayor of Animal Town: Mr. Luckson Jr. and Ms. Camilla. Each will now have an opportunity to speak. We will begin with the first nominee. Mr. Luckson, the floor is yours." Having said this, the bison steps back from the podium and sinks into his seat.

Mr. Luckson Jr., wearing an expensive pinstripe suit with his necktie dangling sloppily below his paunch, rises from his seat, struts across the stage, and takes the podium. Leaning forward, with both paws grasping the podium where so many illustrious mayors stood before him, the weasel delivers his speech.

"I'm really rich," he begins, "and I will be the greatest mayor the Pred Father ever created. I tell you that. I'm proud of my wealth. I earned it. I've done an amazing job. I started off working for my father, you all know and respect, I'm sure. Well, he taught me business from the time I was a pup, and I've grown our family fortune and made it the biggest and best in Animal Town—a real big-time fortune. I'm really proud of my success. I really am. I want the preds of Animal Town to get some shiny rocks too. Not as much as me, of course, but you can still get some. There is so much wealth out there that can make our town so rich again and make it so great again. Because, you know, rich and great are the same thing.

"When prey come to Animal Town from the south, especially the south, but the east too, they bring their problems. They're bringing poverty; they're bringing crime, like that crooked rabbit Jack. They're bringing their weak prey blood. I collect rent at some of our properties. I've seen their filthy shanties. You should see how these filthy prey live, disgusting. How are these animals gonna lead us? How are we gonna go back to the past and make things great again? We can't, not with prey in charge. They can't lead us back to the Promised Land. But I can do it. You know I can do it. How will I do it? I would build a great wall, a big, beautiful wall around the prey shantytown. Nobody builds walls better than me, believe me, and I'll build it real cheap, you'll see. I'll build a great, huge wall all around that trashy prey neighborhood, and I'll make them pay for it. The big wall will stop them from weakening our pred blood; it will keep them separate. I guarantee it.

"And another thing, these prey, you know, they all have like four or five or even six kids. Crazy right? Well, I'm gonna put a tax on prey families with more than two fawns or kits or whatever. That will stop them from replacing us. They will not replace us. Mark my words. And I'm gonna stop prey immigration too, into Animal Town. Count on it. Unless they're rich. If they're rich, maybe they can come, but they have to pay a big tax.

And I'm gonna use the shiny rocks from those taxes, the prey family tax, the prey immigration tax, to give rocks for every pred child and for every pred immigrant. Every pred family will get rocks for each pup they have. And each pred who immigrates from the West will get rocks too. It'll be great. And if there's enough left over, we'll pay prey who are already here to go back to where they came from. We preds are gonna take Animal Town back, big time.

"And one more thing. Last one, I promise. I'm gonna shut down the lyin' Animal Times. That paper and its prey editor, you know, the silly goose, they are public enemies—all their lies about preds. I'm shutting them down my first day as mayor. You watch. That's how we make Animal Town great again, big time. I'm the only animal who can do it. You know I can. Lots of animals tell me that."

His tirade concluded, Junior stands looking from side to side with a smug grin on his face. Perhaps five seconds pass in eerie silence, during which the animals process the torrent of words they have just heard. Nothing like it has been uttered in their hallowed Town Hall before. Then, simultaneously, the animals on either side of the hall react.

"*Bwahahaha!*" Uproarious, mocking laughter bursts from the left. The prey animals toss their heads and slap one another's backs with glee.

"Not even the dumb rural preds would vote for that

clown!" says a deer to a pronghorn.

"Is this a joke?" a pheasant wonders aloud.

They are sure Camilla will be elected mayor now, for they cannot imagine any animal, even preds, supporting such an arrogant, incoherent weasel. But their mirth is stifled almost as soon as it begins by shock, disbelief even, at the reaction of the preds: they are cheering.

The right is shouting, clapping, and whistling with zeal. Howls from dozens of canids fill the hall, punctuated by various animals yelling, "Make Animal Town great again!" and, "You will not replace us!" Delirium grips the preds. Paws stretch out to touch Mr. Luckson as he struts back to his seat, waving his arms in the air. "Watch the suit," he says.

Meanwhile, Mr. Hoofman looks on in despair. His face is ashen. When the commotion finally subsides, he drags himself back to the podium and says, "Ms. Camilla, the floor is yours."

Now the beauteous big horn sheep rises, dressed as usual in a pressed suit and sensible heels. She approaches the podium with a dignified air, carrying a notebook which she opens and places upon it.

"My fellow prey and pred allies," Camilla says, looking as earnest as she can, "we are better than this. What you've just heard from my opponent, that's not our Animal Town. Junior, your comments are hurtful and offensive, and they stir up images of ancestral oppression. How *dare* you? You have no idea how prey have suffered. You have no idea how *I* have suffered. There is not a prey I know who cannot claim to be the victim of some form of systemic specism or discrimination.

"So let's speak an uncomfortable but honest truth: specism is real in Animal Town. This age-old form of hate has been given new fuel by the murder of a hardworking jackrabbit, who only wanted to feed his family, and by the resurgence of pred supremacy preached at the so-called Great Predator Temple. We need to speak this truth so we can deal with it. It is not animal justice to hide behind the fiction of 'equal justice under law,' supposedly blind to species, while condoning murder and condemning Jack for doing no more than he believed he had to. That's *pred* justice. Our justice system needs drastic repair. Let's speak that truth.

"When I am elected mayor, my first act will be to fire Officer Furman and see that he is punished for murdering Jack. Henceforth, only prey will be eligible to serve as police officers in Animal Town. Because there is no such thing as reverse specism, a powerful prey police force will ensure animal justice is imposed on all. Further, I will immediately begin the work of dismantling *and reversing* pred supremacy in Animal Town. I will do this in two ways: first, I will introduce a tax on the wages of all working preds—only revenue from property rents will be exempted. The shiny rocks generated from this tax will be redistributed among all the prey of Animal

Town, regardless of their wealth. Call it blood money for eight generations of oppression. Second, I will radically reform our voting laws to reverse the political exclusion once suffered by prey. Henceforth, pred votes will count for only three-fifths of prey votes. These changes will shift the balance of power in the direction of animal justice for many generations to come.

"Now, to be fair, I agree with Junior on one point. This cannot be an intellectual debate. We must instead trust our emotions and animal instincts. We must *believe* that harm against any one of us is harm against all of us. That is what I call upon my fellow prey and pred allies to do: trust your instincts, not your intellect. We must be united in our belief in, and in our outrage at pred supremacy; for our belief makes it real, and our outrage makes it wrong. My fellow prey and pred allies, our fight is for big, structural change. Our fight is to *change the rules*. So get ready, because change is coming faster than you think."

Camilla flips her notebook closed and smiles with satisfaction. Now it is the prey's turn to cheer wildly and the preds' to boo and heckle as the sheep returns to her seat.

Mr. Hoofman shakes his head and looks at the floor. He seems to be growing weaker by the minute. At length, the commotion subsides, and once more the old bull rises and saunters to the podium, leaning against it to support himself. His official duties are concluded, but he feels compelled to say his piece.

He pulls a wrinkled scrap of paper from inside his coat pocket, takes a deep breath, and reads, "Hate for hate only intensifies the existence of hate and evil in the universe. If I hit you and you hit me and I hit you back and so on, that goes on *ad infinitum*. Somebody must have sense enough and morality enough to cut it off and inject within the very structure of the universe that strong and powerful element of love. If somebody doesn't have sense enough to turn on the powerful light of love in this world, the whole of our civilization will be plunged into the abyss of destruction. Somewhere somebody must have some sense. Animals must see that force begets force, hate begets hate, anti-specism begets specism. And it is all a descending spiral, ultimately ending in destruction for all and everybody. Somebody must have sense enough and morality enough to cut off the chain of hate and the chain of evil in the universe. And you do that by love.

"There's another reason why you should love, and that is because hate distorts reality. You begin hating somebody, and you will begin to do irrational things. You can't see straight when you hate. You can't walk straight when you hate. You can't stand upright. Your vision is distorted. For the person who hates, the true becomes false and the false becomes true. That's what hate does. You can't think right. The symbol of objectivity is lost. If animals succumb to the temptation of hatred, unborn generations will be the recipients of a long and desolate night of bitterness, and our chief legacy to the future will be an endless reign of meaningless chaos."

Mr. Hoofman folds the paper and replaces it in his pocket. The crowd has listened in silence. Junior sits with his arms folded tightly across his chest and a scoffing look on his face. Camilla rolls her eyes.

"Those words were spoken by the great Marcus Prince more than two generations ago," the bison intones. "He spoke them at a time when prey were systematically deprived of political and social rights, when the specism that Ms. Camilla laments was truly rampant. The prey of his time could scarcely have imagined the freedoms that their descendants now enjoy. And yet, despite the oppression and violence prey were subjected to daily, Mr. Prince did not counsel anger, bitterness, or revenge. He did not preach hate, but love. His lesson is all the more timely today, when all that remains to divide us is mutual suspicion, competing historical narratives, and hate.

"The speeches you have just heard represent Mr. Prince's worst fears made real. Blinded to the truth by their hatred for each other, both preds and prey are enslaved by their distorted memories of the past. Yes, *enslaved* by the past. The preds wish to return to an idealized past of their imagination when preds were in charge and prey knew their place. Through the distorted lens of their hatred, they fail to see the truth that the past was not ideal, even for preds, and that all Animals are better off now. Yes, *all* animals are better off now. The prey, for their part, erroneously believe that the past is still present, that they suffered the oppression of their ancestors, that specism has never been worse. Their hatred blinds them to the truth that there has never been *less* specism in Animal Town than there is today, or, at least, there was less until Jack's untimely death last month incited the forces of hatred and blinded us to the truth.

"So I beg you, predators and prey alike, as Marcus Prince once did: let go of your hatred, view the past and the present with the symbol of objectivity, and love one another. For when we turn our tails on the truth, we sow the seeds of our own destruction."

The old bull exhales heavily. He wobbles at the podium. For a moment he is hopeful. Perhaps he has made an impression. Perhaps Mr. Prince's words have once more saved Animal Town.

"Pred lover!" shouts the buck in charge of ATU's Prey Studies Department, puncturing fleeting hopes.

"Species traitor!" Dr. Greenbitter squeaks.

"Marcus Prince was a damned fool, and so are you!" rasps Mr. Scratch.

"Another lyin' prey!" shouts Junior.

"How dare you speak that way about Mr. Prince," says Camilla, glaring at Mr. Scratch.

"Quiet, ewe!" growls Fleischbauer, through clenched teeth.

Mass hysteria rapidly overtakes both sides of the hall.

Wings flap, hooves stomp, and teeth gnash. Rival chants rise to the rafters: "Prey lives matter! You will not replace us!" For the second time in as many days, the species are on the edge of violence.

"No, no. Please, please," Mr. Hoofman is saying, in a vain attempt to soothe the mob. One forehoof grips the podium while the other flails frantically. "Enough, please sto...*p*," escapes his lips as his free arm swings to grip his chest. He loses his balance and keels over, knocking aside the podium with his collapsing bulk. The historic oak artifact tips over the stage and crashes between the aisles, splintering into several pieces. Simultaneously, the prescient bull tumbles over in a heap in the middle of the stage. He lies motionless.

The commotion interrupts the seething animals. Eyes turn toward the stage. "Get a doctor!" someone shouts. Already a ram is making his way out of the row and into the aisle. He is Dr. Woolston, father to Floppy's classmate, Cassie, and a medical doctor at Animal Town Hospital. He rushes to the stage and Mr. Hoofman's side. Other animals soon crowd in. The ram pushes the bison onto his back and feels his neck with one hoof while holding the other over his mouth. One, two, three, four, perhaps ten seconds pass, as the animals look on in stunned silence. Then Dr. Woolston speaks.

"Mr. Hoofman is dead."

CHAPTER 13

Prior to the town meeting and unbeknownst to Mr. Luckson, Junior and Camilla had each struck a deal with the leader of their respective factions to secure their nominations for mayor. In exchange for the zealous fox's endorsement, Junior offered Mr. Scratch a tithe amounting to ten percent of the Luckson Family Corporation's annual revenues. In addition to the anti-prey policies mentioned in his speech, Junior also secretly promised to require magic stories about the Great Pred Father be taught at the former Luckson All Animal School and to use public funds to support the Temple School. Reintroducing segregation by building a wall around the prey shantytown was Mr. Scratch's idea, but Junior readily adopted it as his own, perceiving that it is a concrete, if impractical goal for preds to rally around. Likewise, Dr. Greenbitter extracted a mix of financial and policy promises from Camilla in exchange for her endorsement. In addition to the tax, police, and voting reforms mentioned in her speech, Camilla secretly agreed to appoint Dr. Greenbitter Animal Town's first Retribution Commissioner, giving her the power to review all laws and to veto or rescind those she deems detrimental to prey. Further, using Luckson Family Corporation funds,

Camilla agreed to endow an Anti-Specist Research and Policy Center at ATU. As such, both mayoral candidates stand in need of Mr. Luckson's support to fulfill their campaign promises.

After the town meeting and the impromptu rallies with their partisans that followed, Camilla and Junior make their separate ways to Luckson Manor, hoping to secure their employer's backing. The rival animals chance to arrive at the same time. Under the portico, they nod perfunctorily to each other before being ushered inside by the butler. "The gentle-animals await you in the parlor," says the bison, taking their coats.

Mr. Luckson has remained aloof from the town meeting so as not to risk being exposed by either of his grantees. For his part, Judge Cavendish was obliged to abstain due to the demands of his office. As the official who is to count votes and announce the result of the election, he must appear impartial. The two have spent the evening drinking and smoking in confident comfort.

By the time Camilla and Junior enter the parlor, it is late, and the weasel and lion have drunk several glasses of scotch. Through the haze created by several of the Judge's cigars, the fire casts flickering light onto the aristocrats' animated faces.

"*Guffaw!* We've got them right where we want them now, old chap," says the rotund mountain lion, swallowing another sip of scotch and smiling between rosy cheeks.

"I dare say events have unfolded more favorably even than I planned," replies the wealthy weasel. "The poor of every species are at each other's throats, their leaders are in my pocket, and now my son and consigliere are both nominated for mayor. Aha! And here they are now. Come in, come in. Join the celebration!"

The mayoral candidates exchange greetings with the landlord and judge and take up crushed purple velvet chairs on opposite sides of the fire. "You should have seen my speech, Daddy," says Junior. "I had them in the palm of my paw!"

"Bah!" mocks Camilla. "It was nothing but rambling nonsense. Didn't you hear the prey laughing at you?" Turning to Mr. Luckson, with her chin slightly upturned and her eyelids nearly closed, "Sir, I assure you that my speech carried the day," she says.

"Oh, I've had a full report already," says their employer. "Furry phoned me directly. Too bad about old Hoofman, but what's done is done. More to the point, I must say I commend you both on your initiative. My plan was only to ensure the preds and prey were too busy hating one another to turn their attention on me, but you've done me one better. By winning nominations for mayor, you've guaranteed the Luckson fortune will remain untouched for years to come. Congratulations to you both!"

"I say, bravo!" Judge Cavendish chimes in. "I know I can rely on both of you to protect me from any repercussions of my judgment last month. Together we will uphold the 'powers that be' in Animal Town—powers that be in this very parlor, mind you."

"What makes you so sure you can trust little Camilla not to betray you?" Junior asks impatiently. "She is a lyin' prey, after all."

"I'm more reliable than you, *Junior*, and I've done far more to make the Luckson fortune what it is than you have. Besides, I assure you, Mr. Luckson, as I said at the town meeting today, I will only tax working preds when I am mayor. Landowners such as you won't pay a gram."

"Oh, I do not doubt it, Camilla. I know where your loyalty lies," says the senior weasel. "Nevertheless, I have devised an insurance policy. You see, the judge has been good enough to draft a little document that ensures whichever of you is elected mayor will share my interests in perpetuity." He lifts a sheet of parchment paper from the dark maple side table and holds it aloft. "This states that whoever is elected mayor will be granted executive management and fifty-one percent inheritance of the Luckson Family Corporation. The other will be guaranteed employment with the Corporation and forty-nine percent inheritance. Should Camilla win, I will adopt her as my daughter, and she will be required to take the Luckson family name. So, you see? You both have a powerful incentive to protect my wealth, for in doing so you ensure your own. Rather neat, isn't it?"

"Right-o, old chap," agrees the judge. "And a fine fortune may it ever be, less my trifling fee, of course."

"Oh, I would be honored, sir," gushes Camilla. "Joining your family would be a dream come true."

"What!" Junior exclaims. "You can't adopt that ewe! She's a filthy prey! It would disgrace our pred blood!"

"Hush now, Junior," chides his father. "You really do take such things too seriously. You know that I only stoked animosity between the preds and prey in order to divide and rule them. I bear no real prejudice against the prey, so long as they are well-to-do, of course. It's only coarse working animals I cannot suffer. So far as I'm concerned our family's honor is derived only from the wealth we command. I don't care whether a pred or prey is responsible for increasing that wealth; my only concern is that it does increase."

"But you haven't heard Mr. Scratch speak, Daddy. There won't be any preds left if Camilla gets elected!" pleads his petulant son.

"I have so heard him, and, I must say, I have no time for zealots of any type. He and that gopher schoolmaster are mere tools in my hand. But if it means that much to you, Junior, I suggest that you win tomorrow."

"You'd know there's no chance of that, *Father*," says Camilla, "if you saw what a clown he was this evening. Soon you'll be working for me, *Junior*, so I suggest you get used to the idea."

Junior's eyes redden with rage, and his fur stands on

end. In an instant, he is up from his chair and bounding toward his rival with teeth gnashed and eyes blazing. "I told you not to call me Junior!" he shouts as he bears down on the sheep. Camilla recoils in fear but not before Junior rakes his claws across the flesh of her hind leg, just above the knee.

"*Ba-aaaaaa!*" Camilla bleats in terror, leaping from her chair and seeking refuge behind its high velvet back.

"Let that be a lesson to you, you filthy prey," Junior growls. Blood drips from his paw onto the maple floorboards. "Mark my words, *ewe*; I will see to it that you never inherit my fortune or pollute my noble Luckson bloodline. I'll see that you're locked up when I am mayor, I swear it!"

"I say!" exclaims Judge Cavendish.

"Blast it! That's enough, both of you," commands Mr. Luckson. "I will not let your squabbling ruin my celebration. Have some scotch and calm down this instant."

Camilla composes herself and straightens her rumpled suit. A thin trickle of blood runs down her torn pant leg.

"Thank you, *Father*, but I prefer not to remain in *Junior's* company for a minute longer. Besides, it's late, and I must be returning home. I have an election to win tomorrow, after all. Goodnight, Father. Goodnight, Judge Cavendish."

She turns and makes her way for the door, limping slightly. Junior shouts after her, "Yes! Out with you, and don't come back!" She does not respond and is soon out of sight.

"*Really*, Junior, you must practice moderation, for your father's sake," advises the judge.

"To fire with moderation, and to fire with you! This insurance plan was probably your idea, you species traitor!" Junior turns to his father, and his expression softens. "I'll win tomorrow, Daddy, you'll see. I'm going to be the biggest, best mayor in history!"

Then the portly weasel turns and marches defiantly out of the parlor. Once in the hall outside, he lifts his bloodstained paw to his sensitive nose and inhales deeply. A menacing smile curls across his face. He eagerly licks the blood from his hand, smacking his lips with primal satisfaction.

CHAPTER 14

It is a clear, bright vernal equinox, a day when animals' distant ancestors would shake off the cold and darkness of winter and celebrate the return of warmth, light, and life. It is a day of transition, when the Earth shifts relative to the sun; when animals would feel relief at having come through another winter and look confidently toward the promise of spring. Animal Town's founding fathers chose to hold elections on this day to symbolize the hopefulness and optimism of each new mayoral term. They sought to orient citizens' thoughts toward the future. The passage of time and the birth and death of ten generations of animals have obscured their purpose, however. Today animals merely vote on the first day of spring out of habit. They are fixated on the past, and the spirit of optimism no longer pervades them.

Voting begins promptly at sunrise. A large mahogany poll box sits on a table at the center of Town Square. A steel padlock, to which Judge Cavendish holds the only key, seals its heavy lid, into which is cut a narrow slit. Animals file by to deposit their votes, as statues of their illustrious founding fathers look on. Mayor Blinkin and Marcus Prince join them, looking both serene and troubled, their satisfaction at lives well lived and their concern for work left unfinished immortalized in granite.

Many preds have risen before dawn to make the journey from the countryside, leaving their children to tend the farms. The Luckson Shiny Rock Mine, too, is abandoned today, while the prey employees perform their civic duty. Thus, as the hours pass and the sun climbs toward its zenith, Town Square fills with ever more animals. Too young to vote, only the children of Animal Town are absent.

Having cast ballots, as is becoming instinctual, the species segregate themselves on opposite sides of the square. All but a few preds congregate on the northwest half of the square, closest to the countryside from whence most came. The remainder gathers with the prey on the southeast half, nearest the shiny rock mine and just in front of ATU. Birds and mammals, predators and prey mill about excitedly as they await the outcome of the election.

About mid-morning, as the sun's rising rays dry the dew from the square's greening grass, Camilla arrives, leading a throng of supporters. Dr. Greenbitter is at her side, wearing a fashionable plaid beret that neatly matches her candidate's royal blue suit. Avery is there, too, pointing a video camera at Camilla and asking questions as they approach the poll box. The head of the Prey Studies Department trots behind, alongside school board members and various other leading prey. A cheer rises from the southeast when the herd recognizes its champion. *Vote Prey or Betray!* signs, affixed to wooden stakes, rise and bob over their heads. Camilla and her entourage register their votes and then proceed to press the fur and feather among the gathered prey.

An hour passes. It is nearing midday. The preds grow restless and strain their eyes to look down the streets approaching the square. Signs bearing their slogans flag. "Where is Junior?" they question one another. They do not know that he opted to squeeze in nine holes of golf this morning, for he fears his playing time will be reduced when he is elected mayor.

At length, a luxury car pulls up and parks on the west side of the square. Its vanity license plate reads LUCKSON. A bison in starched suit and tails exits the driver seat and opens the passenger door. Out steps Junior in his standard sack suit and red tie. He is immediately greeted by roars and raucous cheers from the preds. Signs are hoisted. Grinning widely, he strides toward the poll box, chest puffed out and gut sucked in, and is surrounded by animals who believe him to be their savior. Mr. Scratch and Fleischbauer head the pack.

Unnoticed, the Luckson family butler and chauffer trots across the square and joins the prey herd.

Junior is among the last animals to cast a ballot. He does so only minutes before the sun reaches its apex, beaming directly upon the assembled animals and bathing all in white light. The rival crowds murmur in their separate camps. Eyes now shuttle between wristwatches and streets, on the lookout for Judge Cavendish. Tense minutes pass, like those spent at a dying patient's bedside.

Then a siren punctuates the near silence. Officer Furman's police cruiser roars up to the curbside. A fat mountain lion, clad in his robes of office, staggers out. Now all the adult citizens of Animal Town are present, save Mr. Luckson, who awaits the election result in the comfort of his mansion, confident that he shall win regardless of who carries the day. Judge Cavendish appears worse for the wear from a night's drinking and smoking. Carrying a notebook on which to tabulate votes, and with Furman at his side, he slowly walks to the center of the square. Without saying a word, the judge unlocks the sturdy padlock, opens the poll box, and begins extracting the ballots within. Reading each with bleary eyes, he marks his notebook and then places it in one of two piles on the table: Junior on the right, Camilla on the left. The candidates and their supporters watch quietly a few paces distant, smiling or frowning at the placement of each ballot.

This continues until the sun is well past its peak, hastening its decline. At the end of the first count, the two stacks of ballots are too even to judge by eye. Only the black-robed mountain lion knows the tally. But, to be made official, it must be confirmed by a second count. So the process is repeated.

As they await the result, animals spread out upon the square's fresh spring grass. Some enjoy an impromptu picnic. A gopher has brought a pawball, and before long a game is organized. Because hoofed animals make excellent defenders, while those with paws are better on the attack, players are chosen for their skill rather than their species. The result is two mixed teams of both preds and prey. Across a makeshift field spanning both sides of the square, they join a spirited but fairly contested match. Animals cheer them on from the sidelines. For a few fleeting minutes, harmony is restored through the pure objectivity of sport. The game distracts animals' attention from politics and suggests that species can achieve more in concert than in combat. The match is still ongoing when Judge Cavendish is heard to exclaim, "The result is now official!"

By this time the sun is setting on Animal Town. The friendly contest is abandoned, and the mixed teams decompose into opposing tribes. All gather around the judge to hear who has been elected mayor. Camilla and Junior stand nearest, just beside the table where the ballots are stacked. Furred or feathered faces fan out behind them, occasionally obscured by signs on stakes.

The judge rises from his seat behind the poll box and clears his throat. A hush falls over the crowd. "With fifty-one percent of the vote… Mr. Luckson Jr. is elected Mayor of Animal Town!"

Now Animal Town reaps its bitter harvest. Prey faint in

shock; preds leap with joy. A tumult of unbridled emotion ensues. Junior is shouting wildly, "I win! I win! I'm the greatest! I'm the greatest! All hail Mayor Luckson!"

Camilla shakes her head in disbelief, wide-eyed. "It can't be. It just can't be," she murmurs. Fleischbauer and Mr. Scratch dance a jig arm in arm, laughing maniacally. Dr. Greenbitter weeps bitterly, her face buried in her paws. Avery records the scene with his video camera, through bloodshot eyes. Furman leaves his post at the judge's side to congratulate his patron, smiling sharp white teeth and proudly sporting his Distinguished Service Medal. The black bear is too elated to notice the group of animals pushing their way through the crowd, toward the center of the square where Judge Cavendish stands.

There are several young male prey in the gang—mostly bison, deer, and pronghorn. They wear black military-style boots and cargo pants, and one is carrying a sign. Their torsos are likewise shrouded in black sweatshirts bearing one of two slogans: *Prey Lives Matter* or *Anti-claw: We Stomp Preds*. On their faces is steely determination.

They are upon the judge before anyone has time to react. A bulky bison tosses the table to the side, sending ballots fluttering in the air like oversized confetti. As they float to the ground, two whitetail bucks grab the judge's arms. The august lion stammers, baffled, as the deer stretch his limbs wide. The pronghorn toting the *Vote Prey or Betray!* sign tears it from its stake, which has been sharpened to a savage point, and charges the helpless feline. The spear plunges into Judge Cavendish's chest, penetrating his rib cage and piercing his diseased heart.

"That's for Jack the rabbit!" the assassin shouts, wild rage in his eyes. He twists the stake and yanks it out. Hot blood splashes into the pronghorn's face and onto the deer holding the lion's limp arms. They loosen their grip, and the flabby corpse melts to the ground, quivering. Again the pronghorn stabs his victim with self-righteous fury, this time through the rolls of the dead animal's neck, causing a second, less forceful red eruption.

Mere seconds have passed, but already a wave of hatred is rippling through the crowd. Primal screams fill the air. Mouths gape. Eyes sharpen. Nostrils flare. Mr. Scratch and Fleischbauer cease dancing. The brawny wolf springs upon the murderous pronghorn, pinning him to the ground. His remaining claws gouge the assassin's shoulders. His deer accomplices lay their hooves on the wolf in a futile attempt to intervene. But the wolf closes his powerful jaws on the pronghorn's neck. In one swift motion, he tears fatal chunks of the pronghorn's esophagus and jugular. A crimson geyser erupts, drenching the wolf's grey fur and dissipating the pronghorn's hatred in its wake.

Fleischbauer howls with terrible force, dropping the flesh from his jaws. The carnage only increases.

Terror on their faces, Camilla and Dr. Greenbitter attempt to flee, but they are prevented by an onrush of braver animals spoiling to join the fray. All over the square, signs are shorn from their stakes and trampled under hoof and paw.

Rural preds surge forward. Junior stands to the side, shouting and pointing toward Camilla, "There she is! Get her! Kill her! Kill all the prey traitors!" Several wolves, coyotes, and bears rush past to engage the Anti-claw Gang, which forms a defensive semi-circle around the would-be mayor, Dr. Greenbitter, and Avery. A ferocious melee ensues. Animals are gored, speared, and clawed, and the vitality of youth spills wasted upon the earth. Furman barrels in. The bear smashes a pheasant skull between his mighty paws. As the bird brains drip from his claws, a bison in an ATU campus security uniform hooks him with a black horn and rips a long gash across his belly. The bear's pulsing entrails pour onto the grass. They tangle a charging ram's legs, and he crashes to the ground in a bloody heap. Wolves pounce.

All the while, Mr. Scratch is laughing like a mad-animal and staring up at the sky with his arms raised in vain exhortation. "Wreak they justice oh Great Pred Father!" the fox shouts into the void. "The day of judgment has arrived!"

Standing by Dr. Greenbitter's side, behind collapsing defenses, Avery films the internecine war with his camera. At the top-right edge of his frame, he sees a squadron of eagles diving on their position. Avery swings his camera skyward just in time to capture a shot of scaly yellow feet and razor-sharp talons closing around Dr. Greenbitter's skull, one of which gouges her eyeball through her lens-less frames. Blood soaks the gopher's beret, and she emits a piercing scream as the eagle carries her aloft. A second eagle snatches the camera from the goose's grasp, so he follows the wriggling rodent with his own beady black eyes, his neck craning to see over the crowd. He watches in horror as the eagle releases his prey from a height of ten meters, above the steps leading to Animal Town Hall and Courthouse.

Dr. Greenbitter cries and flails pathetically as gravity and fate do their work. Out of her one remaining eye, she just has time to see the sharp point of Lady Justice's righteous sword rising to meet its mark before everything goes dark. Were justice not blind, she would see a young gopher impaled to the hilt upon her impartial blade, her bitterness dying with her.

Mortal terror grips the feathered voyeur. Avery flaps frantically and rises nearly two meters from the ground before a vixen springs after him. The canid's foaming jaws close on one of the fowl's webbed feet, preventing his escape. Still flapping his powerful wings and stretching the fox's sleek body, the goose twists his long neck backward and pecks out the predator's eyes. At the same time, a pronghorn in blood-soaked, black clothes lowers his head and drives his species' namesake into the fox's exposed abdomen. The vixen releases the goose to howl in pain and fear, as blood dyes her white belly to match her body. Freed of the fox's jaws, the goose honks and flaps excitedly. It rises another meter before a sharpened stake, torn from a *You Will Not Replace Us!* sign, sails to meet it midair. The bird falls like a stone, crashing to the ground in a heap with the fatal spear jutting upright from its breast. Its death will go unreported.

Meanwhile, the battle has begun to turn in the preds' favor. Led by Fleischbauer and Scratch, and goaded by Junior, the rural preds have routed the Anti-claw Gang. Though the prey have fought bravely, they cannot long withstand the predators' superior numbers.

Camilla is forced to beat a retreat with the preds hot on her hooves. Leading a thinned heard, she bleats in panic as she flees. Overhead, white-crowned eagles dive bomb the retreating prey, while geese and pheasants do what they can to fend them off. Wounded birds occasionally spiral to the ground to be trampled under hoof and paw.

The pred pack is in bloodthirsty pursuit, barking and growling across the square. But they stop silent in their tracks when they hear howls and roars, mingled with lows, honks, and chirps, propagating through the sticky air from the southeast corner of the square, just in front of ATU. It seems a contingent of predator students and faculty has reinforced the remnants of the prey army. The sheep and her followers filter through the ranks of this last line of defense and then turn to rally against the pursuing preds.

For a moment confusion reigns among the attackers. They are wary to charge their fellow predators. Moreover, their forces are now more evenly matched, and they face front ranks of sharpened stakes pointed in their direction.

Through the twilight, Mayor Blinkin observes the scene. The serenity seems to have vanished from his stony face, leaving only concern for the tenuous union of species he spent his life establishing. If an animal of his quality were mayor today, he might seize this moment of hesitation and use truth and love to extinguish the blinding fire of hatred burning in animals' hearts. He might remind them that all animals are brothers and sisters, equal citizens of a great republic. Alas, no such animal is mayor today.

"Why have you stopped?" shouts Junior, making his way from the rear to the front of the pack. "I ordered you to kill that filthy ewe!" The corpulent weasel is remarkably unscathed from battle. Even his suit and tie remain spotless.

"But them's preds, Mr. Luckson, sir," says a young bear from the countryside, bleeding from multiple flesh wounds. "Didn't the Pred Father say 'pred shalt not kill pred'? I'd sure hate to make him angry."

Junior is about to lay into the impudent bear when a craggy old fox limps out of the front rank and cuts him off, "*I'll* speak for the Great Pred Father. As leader of the Temple, the right is *mine* alone." Mr. Scratch is missing half his left ear and leaning on a spear for support, but he still has fire in his raspy voice. "That commandment only applies to personal disputes, my cub. Killing is acceptable, nay *required*, when it is necessary to preserve the purity of pred blood and to defend the soil of the fatherland. Those animals over there have turned their tails on the

Great Pred Father and forsaken their heritage. They are lower than dust, lower even than prey! It is your duty to show them the mercy of death to prevent them from committing yet more sin."

The simple preds of the rank and file look at one another confusedly, then shrug their shoulders in fatalist acquiescence.

Now the fat weasel chimes in, needing to say the last word. "Right. The Pred Father agrees with my orders, of course. Charge those species traitors and kill every last one of them—no mercy! And I'll give ten kilos of shiny rocks to the animal that brings me the head of that filthy ewe!"

A cloud of dust and insensate flesh rushes toward the mixed pred and prey phalanx. It will be upon them in a few seconds. Standing in the long evening shadow of Marcus Prince, a ewe in a tattered blue suit and a buck in a soiled corduroy blazer address their troops in the fleeting moments of peace that remain. "Now hold fast," says the buck, "and I promise you each a full scholarship! This is your chance at retribution! Leave none alive!"

"Kill the weasel, Junior, and I will be your mayor!" bleats Camilla. "Give them the animal justice they deserve!" She slips behind the front ranks and out of Mr. Prince's bison-shaped silhouette.

Then all is destruction and death.

Three rows of sharpened points, guarding low, medium, and high, stand cactus-like in the face of the enemy. Packed shoulder to shoulder and blinded with fury, the onrushing preds are mercilessly skewered upon them. Viscera pour forth from disemboweled animals, creating a thick burgundy stew. The defenders press forward. The preds slip back, unable to penetrate the bristling rows of pikes.

The rear prey ranks hurl cobblestones, unearthed from ATU's grand promenade, into the mass of pred bodies. Their flight checks the effectiveness of the dive-bombing eagles. Forced back to the ground, the raptors are less skillful warriors. With the sky clear of predators, geese and pheasants soon establish air superiority. They bombard the preds with still more paving stones. Many animals are brained from above in this way, adding to the muck underpaw.

Soon pred enthusiasm falters. They stagger back a few paces from the spears' reach. The animals wielding them let loose a full-throated cheer and step forward over fallen enemies.

Seeing that his side is having the worst of the engagement, Mr. Scratch steps into the breach and faces the dwindling pred soldiers. "The Great Father is testing us, my good preds! We cannot lose if we have faith in him!"

Before the sinewy old fox can turn to face the enemy once more, he is lifted high into the air on the points of ten antlers. The buck in the corduroy jacket tosses his head, flinging the broken body into the midst of the advancing phalanx. Mr. Scratch is immediately trod into the dirt and gore by dozens of stomping hooves and paws. In mere seconds his body is indistinguishable from the pulp.

The fox's death triggers the effect he sought with his speech. Spurred on by vengeance, the preds rally once more with a massive wolf at their head.

"For Scratch and the Great Pred Father!" Fleischbauer roars through crimson-stained teeth, charging at the buck.

More preds are wasted upon the spikes. But they manage to open a small gap in the center of the opposing line. Through it bounds the fearsome wolf, into the grasp of the ten-point buck. They wrestle mightily for several moments, arms wrapped around one another, slipping and sliding in the gore. As they grapple, the wolf manages to bite the buck at the back of the neck, just above the shoulders. With all his hate and might, he squeezes his powerful jaws until tooth meets bone, then nerve. The buck falls limp, glassy eyes bulging and tongue hanging loose. The wolf raises his paws to howl in premature triumph, but the only sound to pass his lips is a faint groan. Another grey wolf, younger and somewhat smaller, though still large for his species, has driven a spear deep into his left ribs. The elder wolf drops his paws upon his killer's shoulders, helpless, and coughs up a thick clot of scarlet. The two wolves are muzzle-to-muzzle. They look into each other's eyes. Just before his consciousness slips away and is lost to the ages, the father recognizes his eldest son, a student at ATU.

At the far end of the line of battle, unnoticed, the few living eagles are working on a slab of granite. They have affixed ropes around Marcus Prince's sculpted horns and are flapping with all their strength in an attempt to topple the statue onto the defensive line below. The birds of prey have just managed to tilt it on its edge when a bear notices them. He shoulders the pedestal with all his weight, knocking the statue free. As it falls, the stone blots out the last rays of fading sunlight, causing the animals in its shadow to look up. Spears snap from their grip, crushed, like the weary bodies that wield them, under the terrible weight of Marcus Prince. His troubled brow comes to rest upon royal blue cloth and red-stained sheep's wool.

With Mr. Prince's fall, the last semblance of order breaks down. Battle lines blur, mix, and whirl into a seething mass of meaningless chaos. Loosed from the bounds of reason, barbarism reigns, as it ever did in the days before Animal Town. Friend and enemy cannot be distinguished. Pred kills pred, prey kills prey, and they kill each other. Nature is red in hoof and paw.

Junior fears for his life. Slithering on his belly to escape the fray, his baggy suit is smeared with mud and entrails, and his red tie is lost in the mire. His only thought is self-preservation. In the dim recesses of his hind brain, he conjures an image of safety: a thick oak door, a dank underground room, rows of shelves with bottles protruding—the Social Club wine cellar. As the slaughter continues in the square, the cowardly weasel withdraws toward the club, unobserved by all but one animal.

On all fours, the fat weasel winds his way across the square, stepping lightly over wrecked animal corpses. He places a paw upon a floppy rabbit ear. Smeared in clotting blood and frozen in agony, the face to which it is attached yet looks vaguely familiar. The weasel stops for a moment to look at it, tilting his head inquisitively. A thought rises to Junior's consciousness. *This rabbit was married to that thief, Jack.*

In near darkness, with the sounds of carnage echoing through the square, the weasel crawls on in the direction of Animal Town Social Club, followed at a distance by a bleeding bison. At length, Junior reaches the club's door, stands, and grips the knob. The door is locked. The weasel is stricken with panic, feeling suddenly exposed. His pursuer watches from mere meters away. A broken spear protrudes from the bison's chest, and blood oozes down the front of his starched livery. The gloom hides the bull from view, though the sound of his gurgling breath betrays him to the weasel's keen ears.

"Who's there?" Junior says frantically, arms stretched before him and eyes darting.

"Good evening, *Master*. It is I, your faithful butler, your chauffeur, your servant, your *slave*," says the bison, spewing pink froth from his mouth. "But I serve no more! No, no, no! My bonds are loosed, and I am free! Who was once slave is now master, you see. I serve no animal now." He laughs wildly.

"Oh, thank goodness you're here," Junior replies, too frightened to understand and unaccustomed to listening to his erstwhile employee. "The wine cellar inside will be safe, but this door is locked. Make yourself useful and smash it down, hurry!"

"I *shall* smash, Mr. Luckson, not because you command it…" gurgles the bull, taking his last, tortured breath. Then he drops on all fours, lowers his head, and charges at the door. Unable to move in time, the weasel is pinned between the bull and the wood, which gives way and sends both animals crashing onto the floor of the social club. It is the bison's first time inside.

"…but because the world is better without you in it," he whispers, rattling speckled foam into the face of the weasel trapped under his bulk. Unable to move and compressed by the bull's dead weight, the weasel struggles for air and life, suffocates, and succumbs.

CHAPTER 15

"Wake up, Floppy. The sun's up," says Charlie, with a note of disquiet in his voice. A ray of light splashes through a crack in the barn door and onto the loft where the jackrabbit sleeps. He rolls onto his back and rubs his blue eyes, blinking. "Ma and Pa haven't come back from town yet, and they're not answering their phones. Hurry up and help me with the chores and we'll drive in to look for 'em."

Wordlessly, the boys water the garden, finish filling the tractor with diesel fuel, and ensure the planter is full with seed. Today Charlie's father was to begin planting this year's crop of high-protein pred grain.

Chores done, the friends are soon bouncing down a gravel road, toward Animal Town. Before long, they reach the city limits. They pass the half-built Great Predator Temple and the field where they played pawball together. The boys note that the pack of predators that usually attends the morning service is curiously absent. Driving on, they pass Marcus Prince Prey Memorial School. The carpenters that have been laboring to expand and improve Dr. Greenbitter's adjacent living quarters are nowhere to be seen.

"Where *is* everybody?" Charlie asks himself out loud.

"Hey, drive by the rock mine, will ya?" says Floppy. "Maybe my mom knows what's up."

But the mine, too, is abandoned.

"My mom's not answering her phone, Charlie. Turn right here. I want to stop by my den and see what's going on."

The den is empty; Floppy's sister and baby brothers are missing. The door stands ajar. Likewise, the streets of the prey shanty town bear no traffic. All is still.

"Something's wrong, Charlie."

"Maybe there was a problem with the election. Let's check the Town Square." He tries to affect hopefulness in his voice, but he, too, is worried. Animal Town is never this quiet.

The adolescent animals drive slowly toward the square, windows down and looking all around—not an animal to be seen. When they are about two blocks away, Floppy, who possesses slightly better hearing, says, "What's that sound?"

"I don't hear anything," Charlie responds.

"It sounds like, like *crying*."

As the jackrabbit speaks, the coyote turns the wheel and rounds a street corner. Now they can see the square through the windscreen ahead of them. Now Charlie can hear. "It *is* crying, Floppy. Look!" He points ahead and speeds to the edge of the square.

Under the mournful gaze of their founding fathers, the two friends see a crowd of weeping animal children. In their midst lie the ruins of Animal Town, the lifeless corpses of all but one of its adult citizens, stiffened overnight into grotesque caricatures of the animals they once were. The boys' former classmates, Ralph, Goldy, Sylvester, Cassie, Becky, and the rest, are all present. The orphans are crying and consoling in turn, without regard for species. Their lamentations fill the air and resound off the buildings surrounding the square.

Floppy and Charlie race in among them, their eyes already welling with tears. When they find their parents' mutilated remains, they sob bitterly and join Animal Town's wake.

In their grief, the young animals seem to lose the power of speech. They blubber uncontrollably, mumble incoherently, or stare vacantly into space. This goes on for several hours until the rising sun heats the mortal gore and the first odor of corruption meets the keenest animals' nostrils.

It is a warm spring day. The stench of decay swells steadily with the power of the sun's rays. Flies appear to gorge on rotting carrion and torment the living. Gradually, alone or in sibling groups of two, three, or four, the animals withdraw from the square, toward the woods and plains surrounding the town. Unspeaking, with eyes downcast and tails between legs, they recede from civilization and revert to the wilderness from whence their ancestors came. The animals no longer walk upright, like men, but instead slink away on all fours or the wing, as their savage ancestors once did. Charlie departs, unable to say goodbye to his erstwhile friend. An hour later, Floppy is last to leave, leading his sister and brothers, sobbing quietly. Only flies and death remain. Animal Town is no more. The republic has died by suicide, and it ends with the whimper of children.

Sometime later, on a hill overlooking a lake, in the ruins of a mansion, an old weasel starves.

With the children gone and the adults dead, the weasel has obtained the object of his life and realized his forefathers' dream; Animal Town, all of it, belongs to him alone. But his conquest is Pyrrhic. Land ownership cannot be the key to wealth, power, and freedom, after all, for the weasel now owns all the land, but his wealth, power, and freedom are gone.

His stores exhausted and incompetent to feed himself, the weasel withers and dies, alone and unmourned. Alone and unmourned. Seated upright in a sumptuous velvet chair, beneath a priceless crystal chandelier, and under the disappointed eyes of his ancestors, the weasel's skeleton collects dust.

EPILOGUE

A northerly breeze carries a faint whiff of clover. Two nostrils in a furry face inhale it with a sniff. The subconscious notion of food appears in a primitive brain. Long, powerful hind legs push off, forcing a lean body in the direction of the smell. Hop, sniff, twitch, hop, sniff, hop. Now eyes can confirm what nose detected. *Green, not blue*, is how men might translate the primal thought that appears. *Eat food.*

Teeth and jaws munch the sweet and sour leaves. Elongated ears stand alert, pivoting independently at the faintest rustle of grass. Eyes dart cautiously from green clover to blue horizon.

A few meters downwind, joints flex, and muscles tense. The breeze carries a different scent to a different set of nostrils. *Food* appears in the brain behind them. Ears and tail lay flat as one paw slowly rises, extends, and lowers a few centimeters upwind. *Silence*, commands the brain. The paws continue to creep stealthily. Whiskers register passing blades of grass.

Hungry, starving, is both animals' constant background thought. They are gaunt with the struggle for existence.

A clawed paw settles on a half-dry leaf, causing a soft crunch. The hunter halts. The gatherer's senses focus on the direction of the sound. *Danger*, says its brain. *Smell, hear, see.* It obeys and does so for several seconds, hind legs spring-loaded. *Nothing. Danger passed. Eat.* The jackrabbit continues munching.

Silence, the subconscious coyote brain commands again. *Move closer.* It stalks with even greater care until its prey is within range.

In a flash of fur, the coyote springs forward and pounces upon the jackrabbit, pinning it to the ground with its forepaws.

Danger! The jackrabbit's brain screams. *Flee! Fight!* Pitiful, high-pitched squeaks escape its gaping mouth. Its hind legs kick out wildly, trying to gore its attacker with its claws. But the predator rolls its prey onto its side.

Kill! its brain commands. The coyote bears down on the jackrabbit's neck. It closes its jaws. A dull snap propagates through the cold.

The hare's body goes limp, and its head rolls toward its attacker, the spark of life yet glowing in its eyes. The animals are mere centimeters apart. Their eyes meet. Simultaneously, atrophied parts of their brains stir. Pulling back from its victim, the coyote cocks its head quizzically.

Flop-py? glimmers through its consciousness. A tear

forms in the corner of the dying jackrabbit's blue eye. *Char-lie?* is its last thought. The withered branches of a perennial idea, long dormant in the untended soil of its mind, die with it.

The predator's instincts resume control. *Eat*, commands its brain, and it eats.

ABOUT THE AUTHOR

A.D. Ultman grew up on a farm on the Great American Plains, surrounded by the species that populate Animal Town. He was educated at leading public universities on the East and West Coasts, studying cognitive science and political theory. He began his career as a U.S. Senate staffer and then spent eight years building and leading a successful corporate market research and consulting practice in Washington, DC. He resigned his position and traveled around the world in 2017. Since then, he has been an independent writer and teacher. He holds a B.S. in psychology and political science and a M.A. in political science.

ACKNOWLEDGEMENTS

The first part of Mr. Hoofman's final speech is adapted from Dr. Martin Luther King Jr.'s 1958 sermon, "Loving Your Enemies."

CPSIA information can be obtained
at www.ICGtesting.com
Printed in the USA
LVHW020504150221
679326LV00003B/284